MEDICINE DOG

MEDICINE DOG

GEOFF PETERSON

ST. MARTIN'S PRESS

new york

MEDICINE DOG. Copyright © 1989 by Geoff Peterson. All rights reserved. Printed in the United States of America. No part of this book may be used or reproduced in any manner whatsoever without written permission except in the case of brief quotations embodied in critical articles or reviews. For information, address St. Martin's Press, 175 Fifth Avenue, New York, N.Y. 10010.

Design by Judith A. Stagnitto

Library of Congress Cataloging-in-Publication Data

Peterson, Geoff.
    Medicine Dog.
      p.   cm.
    "A Thomas Dunne book."
    ISBN 0-312-02949-7
    I. Title.
PS3566.E7687M4 1989   813'.54—dc19   89-30167

First Edition

10 9 8 7 6 5 4 3 2 1

For Rabbit and the kids,
who know more about Boyd Sherman
than anybody

MEDICINE
DOG

ONE

▼▼▼▼▼ IT WAS AFTER FOUR when Boyd Sherman looked up from his chess problem. Wind banged against the trailer, rattling the storm windows. Ice sheeted the inside panes; stalactites hung from the sills. By paying close attention he could make out the wind actually moving some of the taller chess pieces.

"What's that, Buck?" he asked the dog under the chair. Buck was an old Chihuahua he'd gotten in Phoenix; that was before Adrian. Adrian whom he had married and followed to this godforsaken country. Adrian had hated the dog's guts. "Take that wussy with you," she'd hollered. That was the night he couldn't stand it anymore, the night they'd fought. It was during the weekend between summer and winter. He didn't know then how cold it could get. Adrian had tried telling him. "You call this cold?" she'd said. "By November you'll be begging for mercy."

After New Year's the temperature went to fifty below and stayed. Some kind of record.

He wasn't sure if the wind was out to kill him or just drive him crazy. It sounded like a haunting, like a huge engine or a beast growling. He watched Buck for signs but the dog lay seized with shivering, ears back and his one good eye stark and pleading, the other clouded with cataract. His tail lay wrapped around his rear legs. He'd been that way since coming to Wyoming. "Grow some hair," Boyd ordered.

The front door opened in the hall. He could tell because of the ice cracking and the sudden gust under his office door. It was too late for United Way to be snooping around, and the cleaning lady didn't come till six.

At last, he thought, his first client. Missing Persons, a homicide even. The miners were always getting drunk and shooting each other or their wives.

He was scraping chess pieces into his middle drawer when the door opened. "You Boyd Sherman?" she barked.

"Yes," he said. "Please have a seat."

Instead she stomped in place, knocking snow off her enormous mucklucks. When she lowered the hood of her parka, her hair was knotted in pink rollers. Scotch tape pressed a matching set of curls to her temples. For eyebrows she had two penciled shadows that arched above where the real ones were coming in. Her skin was so mummified she looked like a man-thing blown in from the Siberian wastes. Her eyes were two flinty slits nearly obstructed by cheekbone. When she spoke, her lips hardly moved.

Clutched in her mitten was a wad of papers. They looked legal. She shoved them into his chest and he tossed them on the desk and wondered if he should thank her or what.

The woman adjusted her hood and left in a rush of down and nylon. A moment later he heard a door slam, the engine rev and the gears grinding. He went to the hall window and watched her maneuver in the drifts. It was a Dodge Power Wagon at least thirty years old. In front sat a Siberian husky, mute, his milk-blue eyes staring.

• • •

They were from Adrian, or rather her lawyer. Boyd spread the papers on his desk and read each one. Adrian was really divorcing him. He rolled back in his chair and listened to his breath. The wind was somebody else's breath, he thought. Some cold sober sonofabitch who'd been waiting for Boyd Sherman a long time.

The third marriage was supposed to be charmed. Hell, they'd fought about everything. Kids was one issue. He didn't want them. Wyoming was another. He didn't like it. And not getting a job hadn't helped. Finally she got tired of his leaving. He was always leaving. "Go," she'd said. "I mean it."

"I'm leaving," he had announced.

Now he couldn't afford to leave. "Shoulda been here two years ago," the natives said. They referred to the boom like it was a change in weather. People had come to Medicine Dog in waves. Both the mines and the oil fields were humming red-hot seven days a week, sucking in one shift while spewing out another. Late at night you could still hear the buses growling through the empty streets, picking up miners huddled on corners, gripping their six-pack lunch pails. Families bought tract homes, four-wheel drives, and rifles. They shot antelope. They went north to ski.

Then, as it had happened over and over in cycles running back more than a century, the screws popped. It was as though someone had made off in the night with the battery to the place. The charge was suddenly missing.

Desperate, Boyd had decided to go into the detective business just before Christmas. He'd figured it out. With the bust in place, there'd be an increase in disappearances, husbands on the lam with a paycheck and another woman, not to mention robbery and assorted battered wives. Divorce was up. And he'd always been handy with a camera. And besides, there was no other private investigator in Clearwater County. He'd checked the yellow pages.

So where was the business?

The door again.

Boyd crumpled the divorce papers and stuffed them in his desk. When he got to the hallway he saw no one, just the front door wafting and snow blowing in little flashes of crystal. In order to lock it he had to pick at the ice inside the jamb with a butter knife. The wind forced the door against him with the weight of a large man. Finally he had to go outside to get at the ice. He chipped at the hinges until he could stand it no more. Enraged, he kicked the door. It would never be warm again, he swore. Nature was beating back life on the planet. Now was the great reclamation. In Wyoming it had already begun. The land lay scoured like a burnt match. Wyoming, where even the gnarliest perseverance yielded nothing.

At his feet was the latest issue of the Medicine Dog *Stampede,* frozen solid as a log. Boyd whacked it against the jamb, slammed the door shut, and locked it. In the kitchen he turned the oven to 300° and set the paper inside.

The trailer was one of the reasons he had decided on private investigation as a means of income after Adrian. Running the length of a railroad car, it was cheaply partitioned into three offices, baths, a kitchenette, and living room. Despite frozen pipes and the snow drifting under the door, the place looked reasonable. Seventy-five bucks a month bought the exclusive use of a cubicle just big enough for a cot and a desk. He shared a bathroom with United Way, whose office was just next door in the hall. The bathroom had doors to the right and left of the commode, leading to both offices. It also featured a sink and a bathtub–shower containing broken storm windows and assorted agency posters. There was a mirror edged with phony gilt, which the cleaning lady kept spotless. The room reeked of cleaning products that she set in a row under the sink. The porcelain was always slick with polish and his papers always stuck to his desk. A larger office was occupied by the YWCA. That one came with its own bathroom.

Another special feature was the phones. Both United Way and the Y had them. Boyd suggested renting an extension off one of their lines but was told that was impossible. He was, however, permitted to take business calls on the Y phones. The only problem was that he had not gotten one call, business or otherwise, in a month. Once the volunteer supervisor heard him in his office talking to Buck and called the cops. She thought he was a burglar.

The kitchen contained a sink, stove, and refrigerator. The sink had been dry ever since the pipes froze. That went for the toilet too. He liked the kitchen when the place was empty because the light on sunny days shot through the big window, heating up the room. He'd sit at the table, smoke cigarettes and read the paper. That was before the women complained of the smoke. Now there wasn't even water to make coffee.

Another reason for becoming a private investigator was the newspaper, which was now cooling from the oven. The *Stampede* was a weekly rag that solemnly swore to report no story not containing the name of at least one local resident. Last August, Boyd, equipped with resumé and a file of his work, had asked for a job. The editor, a man half his age, explained the situation. "Here's our situation, Floyd," he'd said. "Most work here is on a volunteer basis. We might have an opening in Obit that might lead to something. But I can't promise."

Just the year before, Boyd Sherman had been a prize-winning sports feature writer for the Phoenix *Sun*. He didn't cotton to a rich kid in a monogrammed blazer offering him Obit. In fact it infuriated him. "Eat this rag," he'd transmitted telepathically.

The Phoenix *Sun*, now there was a newspaper. That's when he was still drinking and he and McLaren understood each other. McLaren was the best senior editor in the Southwest. McLaren had made him what he was. Just four years ago Boyd Sherman had broken the story about pro football coming to Arizona. The following spring he won the Press Club award for a series investigating allegations of drug payoffs to college athletes in the Pac-Ten. The story got picked up by the wire services. He appeared on radio and TV. He was offered an advance to write a book.

Then the unthinkable happened. The drug scandal cooled and the deals fell through. Finally, with only the Scottsdale horse auction to write about, he drank. He outdrank McLaren, outdrinking even himself in the end when he collapsed in the city room, taking out a solid two-hundred–pound teletype on the first try. McLaren didn't squawk. He covered for him in the publisher's office and made Boyd promise to keep writing no matter what. "Sell newspapers," he'd ordered.

Instead, Boyd sobered up. He went to treatment for three weeks and when he returned, things at work changed. McLaren no longer had time to talk. There were fewer assignments. When Boyd confronted him one day in the men's room, McLaren exploded, accusing him of sloughing off, of not pushing a story the way he used to, that he no longer "made" stories—that was his word. "What happened to the killer who used to write for me?" he yelled.

When Boyd objected, he was given the high-school swim scene.

"I quit," Boyd announced.

Back at the apartment Boyd drank diet pop, waiting for Adrian. Adrian was twenty going on forty-five. Boyd wasn't sure what that meant except that she made decisions, not rashly, but she didn't wait for things to make up her mind either. She'd been studying geology at the U. but decided to quit when they got married. They honeymooned in Vegas during final exams. It was the only time he could get away.

While in Vegas he got the news. McLaren the SOB had fired him because he was sober, how do you like that? McLaren had lost his best drinking buddy. But not to worry. Boyd had been thinking of some new lines of work. Hell, he was literate and could talk to people, and these days skills like those were at a premium. He'd make some phone calls.

"But right now, come here," he had said.

Adrian stood staring out the window at Vegas blazing in the late afternoon while he undid her buttons. "I'll get a job at K-Mart," she'd offered.

That wasn't exactly what he had in mind. He wanted to fix everything, to make himself better, there, on the pile carpeting. He wanted to be taken by her and covered over. Vegas was the beginning of the end, he'd thought.

Wyoming was home to Adrian even though her dad barely spoke to her. Vern Chessley hated Boyd's guts, that much was clear. When Adrian introduced Boyd as a prize-winning journalist, Chessley had asked, "What prize?"

Vern Chessley was a high-plains sheep herder who found most men's handshake suspect. To him, Boyd was a drifter without values because he was nearly twice Adrian's age, period. The old man eyed him with a mixture of pity and disgust, as if his son-in-law had never learned to play poker or talk man-to-man.

Boyd didn't warm to Vern Chessley either. He tried telling Adrian it was no use, to just accept the old bastard and go on with her life. That was a mistake. Adrian, to her way of thinking, *was* getting on with her life. Adrian was home; it was Boyd who was the stranger, who would never understand men like her father. "Men like Vern made this country," she often insisted.

Vern Chessley had buried his wife after forty years of marriage. Once Boyd visited the grave with Adrian, a lone wooden marker at the foot of a butte. "You see this place," Adrian had said. "The Indians used to stampede the buffalo to their deaths here. They'd run them off the cliff, take what they needed, and leave the rest."

Boyd sat in the kitchen, wrapped in a blanket, and lit a cigarette. Cold was the scariest, he thought, turning the oven up high. Before the pipes froze he'd cup his hands to his coffee, hunched over at the table reading "Dear Abbey," his horoscope, anything. Now it was dark and by the fluorescent light he couldn't tell if it was smoke from his Pall Mall or his own breath. Fifty below zero. It wasn't even funny anymore. Adrian would find him curled in the bathroom, the coffee can filled with urine frozen to his hand. They'd make up stories about him and no one would claim the body.

"Dammit," he said. The oven element was shot. The ice from the *Stampede* had shorted it out. Everything broke down. Winter was a gradual stripping away, he'd always known that. He balled the paper in his fist and retired to his office.

Sitting at his desk, he decided to look for work the next morning. He checked it on the wall calendar. January was the worst, he thought. And it didn't get better. They all said it would get better; the guys in treatment said it got better. But it didn't.

He blew on his hands and began reading. HORSES MISSING; STILL NO CLUES, said the front page. The locals had a problem. Last October a dozen prize-winning horses were stolen from the city corrals. Police Chief Everett Follet had been quoted as saying it was a professional job. That is, it was done in the middle of hunting season when most self-respecting families were out killing Bambi. When nothing turned up, the citizens got riled. At a city council meeting they'd accused Follet of incompetence. One respected council member had called him a horse thief.

Then it was discovered that horses had come up missing in a number of towns in three surrounding states. By Christmas, state and federal agencies had been alerted. Chief Follet's answers to reporters became even more cryptic. "We've reason to suspect a conspiracy," he'd said.

STILL NO CLUES, said the paper. Biggest crime of the half-century. Wyoming, Colorado, Idaho, Montana, who knew where it would stop? Put out an all-points. Boyd imagined Vern Chessley raising hell at City Hall—that he'd read about it in the *Stampede* and come all the way in from his ranch, steaming up the windshield of his Bronco with his rage, aiming his fat, scaley finger at Chief Follet and declaring, "Sheep'll be next."

The city council had long wanted the corrals shut down but couldn't get the citizen support to do it. They're an eyesore, the council had claimed. They'd called them a health hazard. Now it seemed to some citizens that the council had finally resorted to crime and bad publicity to accomplish their goal.

Others said it was a plot by the Bureau of Land Management to kill off the wild horses. Shut down the corrals and the sale of the mustangs would drop off, they reasoned. That way the BLM got to stop its annual capture and sale of the horses. Next step, extinction. The federal boys were in cahoots with the big energy conglomerates, they said.

"Cowboys," Boyd snorted, tossing the paper. He was about to rejuvenate his chess problem when he heard water running. He swiveled in his chair and glanced at the floor. Buck was taking a leak on the Medicine Dog *Stampede*, too cold to even lift his leg.

"Grow some hair," Boyd growled.

TWO

▼▼▼▼▼ AFTER A COLD NIGHT'S sleep, Boyd found a note under his door. He'd gotten a call.

"I'm Boyd Sherman," he said, entering United Way. "You're new."

The girl behind the desk looked startled. "Hi," she said.

He held up the note. "Male or female?" he asked.

"Female."

"Leave a message?"

"She said she'll call back."

Adrian, he thought. What did she want? He tried calling but got no answer. You couldn't tell when she'd be home ever since she'd got on at the trona mine. When they first broke up he'd imagined her in bed with some big guy from the mine, some ex-Marine with horror stories about 'Nam. He'd imagined Adrian and her leatherneck watching muff films on the VCR, naked the whole long-change between shifts. In his mind he'd even named him. He could hear her say it. "Jack. Oh, Jack."

God, he hated trona, the raw white mineral from the mines that went into making glass. In town it lay in piles on the railroad sidings where the cars had leaked. Everything wore a fine, silty coat of it. The papers on his desk were gritty with it. Trona, coal, oil, it was all the same. All that wealth sunk in what they called the "Overthrust," the geological warp that slashed the state like a huge dinosaur tongue. Bumper stickers boosting trona read *Only the Best Comes in Glass*. Boyd drank Coke out of cans.

Ten already. Not wanting to be late for his appointment with Chief Follet, he dressed, fed Buck, then wrapping the army blanket about himself like a shawl, wheeled his bike outside. "I'm going to the PO," he hollered.

It was a three-speed he'd paid ten dollars for at the police auction last fall. He'd gotten it for exercise. Then came the first blizzard and the separation from Adrian. Now the bike was his sole means of conveyance. He'd put a basket in front and reflectors fore and aft. It needed brakes, however. A week after he'd bought it he discovered the cable cut.

Cut your cable, he'd thought. It sounded like a vasectomy.

Downtown was quiet. On the streets icicles hung from power lines. In the sun's glare the air crystallized and fell down, stinging his face. Breathing made him choke. When the wind didn't gust, it almost felt warm.

That was dangerous. Desert air was as treacherous as a mirage. It came suddenly and attacked the body's thermostat. It gave you ideas that didn't jibe with the facts. Alone, you could die crossing the parking lot.

Wyoming was called the "Equality State" because in winter it was impossible to tell the men from the women. Thick fur, down parkas, and wool muffled the body's curves. Not even the cops knew for sure. Only miners who'd worked a few winters could tell the difference. They'd zoom around Safeway's parking lot in their pickups and whistle at some amorphous hulk loading groceries into her Suburban. When a miner whistled, you knew it was female. It was a perception bordering on telepathy.

In winter families stuck together and raised kids who went to schools named after presidents no one had ever heard of. There was a small-town pride in the place. People attended meetings. Boy Scouts, NRA, and church socials dotted the calendar every Wednesday in the *Stampede*. What prevented Medicine Dog from becoming a real town was the absence of a stable population. Not since the heyday of the railroad had people actually spent their lives here. Most locals harbored a secret ambition to return to their real homes back East as soon as the economy picked up there. Some had been waiting ten years.

The town's chief winter sport was playing video tapes. Shoppers got fat on too many groceries just to pick up on the free tape offers. At the Mini-Mart, buy ten gallons of gas, rent a movie free. On especially grim weekends the video outlets offered "Socked In Specials." Toons for the kids, a half-dozen "major motion pictures," and a couple sleaze reels for the man of the duplex.

That's what the drinking and battering were all about. The disease was cabin fever and Boyd Sherman had it in stereo. Maybe all the movie freaks were right, he thought. Maybe we were closer to Hollywood than to reality. Maybe it was saner to just stay indoors and dream.

The sign on the bank said minus forty. Meanwhile, at the corner of Utah and Railroad four hundred sheep went through a red light. Basques on horseback herded them across the overpass on their way to winter grazing. Police cars blocked the intersection.

The Basques had raised sheep in these parts for decades. Basques didn't have TV. They were real shepherds and like the ones in the Christmas story stayed on the outskirts and knew the stars.

"Beautiful morning," said the cop. "Can I see some ID, sir?"

Boyd loosened the blanket around his head and reached for his wallet.

"Boyd, that you? Hell, I thought you was a freight bum. I'm Skeeter."

"I know."

"It's cold," said Skeeter. He looked around, preoccupied with the dispatcher on the radio. Then he squinted up at Boyd. "I'd give you a lift but you're sober."

That winter Chief Follet had initiated a program to get drunk drivers off the streets. The plan was to answer calls from bars and direct a black-and-white to pick up and deliver the inebriate to his home. No charge, no questions asked.

The only problem was that no one called. After New Year's the only drunk to take advantage of the offer was Boyd, and he wasn't drunk. In fact he didn't have an outfit. In Wyoming an outfit wasn't something you wore; you drove it.

He'd go to the Happy Trails and drink Coke till midnight, then call the station. "I'm Boyd Sherman," he'd say. "I'm at the Trails."

That gave him thirty seconds to get into character. Skeeter or one of the others would find him slurring his thank-you's and stumbling over chairs.

In the black-and-white he'd talk about women and the lousy weather. Sometimes they'd talk about the patrol, local politics, unsolved cases. Besides getting around on bad nights, Boyd figured that taking advantage of Follet's service might pay off.

"Playing chess with the chief again?" asked Skeeter.

"If I can make it."

"Well, stay outta trouble."

At the post office he parked his three-speed behind a newspaper machine and checked his mail. People passed him, nodded, then nodded again on their way out. Too cold to talk, folks saw each other out of the sides of their heads and snorted like horses. Sometimes two old guys at the counter talked about beef prices. On windy days magpies waddled around the lot too afraid to fly. By the time they'd get airborne they'd be in Nebraska.

No mail again. Of course no one knew where he was. Just last month he'd received a coupon marked occupant. It was for personalized name stickers.

He was clasping his blanket under his chin when the woman approached him. "Boyd Sherman?" she'd said. "My name's Landrus."

She lowered the hood of her parka and shook out her blond hair. She looked good. She also looked married.

"Your office told me I'd find you here."

"Mrs. Landrus," he nodded.

"Does that name mean anything to you?"

"Landrus, Landrus . . ."

"Rusty's my husband."

He watched her a second then nodded. "Oh," he said.

"Yes."

"I see."

He'd never heard the name before in his life. But that didn't matter. Already he'd sniffed his first case and decided to follow this woman anywhere.

"Can we talk?" she asked.

It was a gleaming black Ford pickup lifted eight feet off the deck with chrome roll bar and searchlights. It sat in the middle of the lot grumbling angrily.

"Just put it in the back," she said, meaning the bike. In the short box were three bales of hay.

He hoisted himself up, slammed the door, and relaxed in a sudden gush of heat. "This is nice," he said.

"It's Rusty's." She poured coffee from a thermos and offered it. "He was a volunteer deputy sheriff."

Inside the cab it smelled like she'd just washed her hair. "Mind if I smoke?" he asked.

"Suit yourself."

"A deputy," he said, trying to pick up the thread. He noticed a leather bag with an eagle feather sticking out of the top. It hung from the rearview mirror.

"Volunteer," she answered. "Rescue calls, mostly. Pulling folks out of drifts. Dragging the river. Last summer, remember when that boy drowned? Rusty was part of that. They do good things."

She suddenly became quiet. She gripped the wheel, her eyes squinting against the sun. Then she looked at him. "So what do you think?"

She wasn't asking for his thoughts on volunteer deputies. "I'm sorry?" he said.

She eyed him critically for a second. "I've never done this before," she said. "I guess you realize that."

"I understand."

She'd removed her thermal mittens and was now tapping the back of the seat. "So what do I do?"

"Just start at the beginning," he said.

She surveyed the traffic on Utah, then cleared her throat like she was about to address a jury. "Rusty and I keep horses," she began.

Horses again. "I see."

She poured more coffee and began telling about a young couple from the Midwest who had decided to put off having kids and raise horses instead. Rusty'd got on at Crater mine and that had left her free to pursue her first love. She trained horses. She didn't break horses like some cowboys did. She bought good horses that challenged her and took time. She took her time about horses.

She and her husband had rented stables down at the corrals. That was when she came out with it. Rusty had been missing since the rustling incident at said corrals.

"Missing?"

"Disappeared," she said matter-of-factly. "Been three months now."

That was the part Boyd was supposed to have already known. He nodded, signaling her to continue.

"The police haven't found anything. So I thought of a private eye."

"And I'm the only show in town."

"You're the only one in the state besides some old geezer in Cheyenne. I checked."

By now his cigarette burned his fingers. He found the ashtray but it was full of change. "Use the window," she said. He tried cracking it but it was frozen. Finally he hit the handle with the butt of his hand and it snapped off in his lap. "Sorry," he said.

She glanced at the handle, then at him. When she didn't speak he thought it best to continue.

"Tell me," he said, "when's the last time you saw your husband?"

"The day it happened."

"The day what happened?"

"The horses."

Boyd opened the door and flicked his cigarette. Rusty Landrus was nothing but a pretext for talking about horses. This woman championed the beasts like they were a social cause.

"Find my husband," she said.

Boyd scribbled his name and message phone on an envelope he took from the dash, tore it off, and offered it. "My card," he said. Then he took her number. "I'll be in touch."

17

"Don't you want to see the stables?" she asked.

Boyd flipped the envelope over. It was addressed to Clyde Paulos, City Hall, Medicine Dog, Wyoming. The return address was a printed sign, a symbol. It was a simple cross with an "S" on the bottom and crowned with a star. "Not now," he said sagely.

"Oh." She sounded hurt.

"I have an appointment," he explained. "At City Hall."

"Can I give you a lift?"

"Thanks."

She leaned over and switched on the tape deck. A country-western crooner whined like a man jumping forty stories to his death. It sounded like he'd changed his mind.

Suddenly Boyd didn't like the looks of the road, the way it came at the windshield in a blur. "Mrs. Landrus," he yelled.

Within seconds she pulled up across from City Hall. There she swerved and whipped the truck in a clean U-turn that set them abruptly on the curb rocking in front of the department's glass doors. She reached over and flicked off the stereo. "The name's Jennifer," she said.

THREE

BOYD ENTERED THE STATION holding Jennifer Landrus's window handle like it was a piece of evidence. There was no place to set it.

Linda the secretary snatched up the phone, punched a button, and announced his arrival. "Chief's in," she said flatly, hanging up.

Strolling past the illuminated drug display, he could peek into every office in the place. Cops sipping coffee from Styrofoam cups looked up.

"They hate me," he thought.

He was an extravagance in the company of men, a drunk who had the chief under his spell with his silly chess. It made him feel guilty to beat Follet every afternoon, especially since the chief was the only one who knew his secret.

Follet didn't mind Boyd's using the department as a taxi service. "Just don't tell me," he said. He knew a lot about Boyd Sherman. For instance, the exact date he'd signed in for treatment for his alcoholism. "Have to run a check on ya," he'd warned on learning of Boyd's intention of taking up private investigation. Boyd felt a rugged brand of respect from this man and he worked at returning it.

"You're late," growled Follet.

The big guy sat hunched at his desk wearing a .38 shoulder holster and brooding over a chessboard set to begin. It was always like that. Follet called him Kimosabe. It made him feel some of his old strength returning.

"Where you been?"

Boyd took his seat in front of the desk and set his window handle in Follet's ashtray.

"What the hell is that?" the chief asked.

"It's a window handle."

"I can see that, but what is it?"

Boyd grabbed two pawns from the board and held them behind his back. When he held his two fists out he was smiling.

"Left," said Follet.

Boyd opened his hand. Black.

"What are you grinning about?" asked Follet, turning the board around. "This blows my whole strategy, you know that?"

Boyd moved first. "Pawn to King four," said Follet, scribbling on a steno pad. Chief Follet, a recent convert to chess, had just learned notation. Recording each move had become an obsession. It took more of his attention than did the prospect of his next move. "Standard opening," he mused, nodding like a grand master.

"I got my first client," Boyd announced.

Follet moved his King Knight. "Congratulations. Who is she?"

"Why *she*?"

"Come on. Unless it's a divorce and nobody gets divorced in this weather. Knight to Bishop three. Am I right?"

Chief was right. Chief played by the rules. A wizened old LA detective for ten years before coming to Medicine Dog to raise his kids, Chief had authority.

"Name's Landrus," said Boyd.

"And she wants to find her husband."

Follet had moved but did not look up to inquire further.

"Yeah," Boyd replied.

Boyd cleared out his King side. Next his Queen would attack Chief's Bishop Pawn and mate in two moves.

"Bishop to Queen four," mumbled Follet.

"Dammit," said Boyd, slapping his head.

Chief glanced frantically at the board. "Where, where?" he said.

"I left my bike in her truck."

"That was dumb, Sherman."

"Can I use your phone?"

"If you think you can without messing up."

Boyd got a busy signal while inspecting the board. Chief was buried up to his ears and didn't see it, he thought. One move and everything would tumble: the chief's King trapped by his own men, hemmed in for ambush. Checkmate; pitiful.

"Hang up," said Chief.

Boyd stared at the receiver, then hung up.

"It's always busy," explained Follet. "She keeps it off the hook. The lady's spooked."

"What about?"

"Who knows? It's your move."

Queen captured Pawn. "Mate," said Boyd.

Follet stopped breathing while he appraised the situation. Finally he nodded. "That's a mate, all right." He looked up and grinned. "Pretty sneaky."

Follet started setting up a new game. "You want a coat?" he asked.

"A what?"

"That one," he said, pointing to the coat tree beside the door. On it was a silvery down parka with a furry hood and enough zipper pockets to smuggle Chihuahuas through Nogales.

Boyd got up and tried it on. "Whose is it?" he asked.

"Hell, it even fits," growled the chief.

Boyd admired himself in it, then hung it back up. "Where'd you get it?" he asked.

Follet was trying out different openings. "Don't ask."

Boyd sat down and opened Pawn to King four. "Thanks," he said.

Follet waved it off. "Just don't tell nobody where you got it."

They played three moves. "So what's she scared of?" asked Boyd.

"Who, Mrs. Landrus? Who knows? Women are screwier than ever. They don't know what they want. They want to be cops. You know what I think? Her husband knows something about horse rustling. And that means *she* knows something. But damn if she'll tell us."

"Tell me about Rusty," Boyd said.

"Not much to tell. He's a truck driver out at Crater. He drives that pickup whose handle you own and lives in one of those hundred-thousand–dollar cedar jobs on south hill. And they're paid for. How he does that on what he makes at the mine is open for discussion."

"Where's he from?"

"Illinois, someplace like that."

"Maybe he went home."

"Yeah, and maybe Clyde Paulos said boo."

"Clyde Paulos? The city councilman?"

The same. The same Paulos who called Follet a horse thief at the last council meeting. The same Paulos who owned the Mustang Cafe.

Chief looked up. "You didn't hear a thing, got it?"

Boyd nodded.

"He's a friend of the Landrus family."

When Follet spoke he meant business. Still it was hard to tell.

"You mean—"

22

"That's all I'm going to say."

"Exactly how much are those missing horses worth?" asked Boyd.

"Five, ten thousand each," said Follet. Then he shook his head. "Naw, he's small time."

"What did Landrus used to do? Cowboy?"

Follet grinned. "She tell you that? Maybe that's what he wanted to be when he grew up but that's jerking off. Horses are money, that's all. It's business."

He pushed back his chair and patted his pot belly. His belt buckle spelled "Chief." "Now Jennifer Landrus, she knows horses."

"Rodeo queen."

"You watch out, she'll make you forget you're married."

"I'm almost not."

Boyd tossed the papers on the desk and Follet snatched them up. Follet liked official papers. He moved his lips when he read.

"Divorcé," boomed Follet. He was doing his impersonation of Judge Broom, known locally as Jug Broom, alcoholic, presiding.

"I now pronounce you free and broke."

"Free and broke," echoed Boyd, raising his Styrofoam cup.

They laughed until Boyd said checkmate. The chief became quiet, glanced at his pad and said, "I forgot to write it down."

Follet fell to adjusting some pieces, creating problems for the white King. "Sorry to hear that, Kimosabe."

"Yeah."

"It's the hardest thing we ever do. Be married, I mean. Me and Emma been together eighteen years going on. We were sealed in the temple. You know what that means, don't you? Means we're together for all eternity. At least that's the idea."

"Yeah."

"Five kids on what I make? Four's enough."

Boyd nodded; he'd heard it before. "Yeah," he agreed. He

took a bite out of the cup and chewed. "My dad died of cancer," he said. "You would have liked him. His name was Ralph and he sure liked to fish."

"Oh yeah?"

"Last time he got sick I went home to see him, back in Wisconsin. We went ice fishing, just the two of us. It was Valentine's day and cold but you couldn't stop him. Mom fixed us a lunch and made me promise to bring him back before dark. Gertrude, that's my mom's name, she's dead now. 'Gert, leave us alone,' my dad said.

"'Someday I will,' she said, 'and that'll be the end of you.'"

Follet laughed and shook his head as if to say, "My, my, such folk wisdom."

"Right then my dad knew the truth. He was dying. The doctors had told him but he just hadn't accepted it. But right then it clicked on inside him like a light. I asked him how he was doing and he said fine. Fine, that's all, like he'd already left his body.

"At the lake we cut a hole and fished it together. There's big pike in there; I used to fish it as a kid. That day I hoped we'd catch something but it didn't happen, not even a nibble."

The phone rang. Or rather it whistled like a goofy tropical bird. The chief gobbled up the receiver, then realized it was the intercom. "I said no calls," he barked.

"It's Lieutenant Frampton," Linda said.

Follet glanced up at Boyd. "Put him on."

The chief punched the flashing button, cradled the receiver under his double chin, and swiveled in his chair to face the wall.

"Chief here." He listened a few seconds, then nodded. "Okay, stay up there and I'll get back later," he ordered and hung up.

"He's my inside man on that horse-rustling matter," said Follet. He glanced at his watch. "Finish your story and get outta here."

"You're busy," said Boyd.

"Finish your story. You're fishing the lake but don't catch anything."

Boyd stood and picked up his window handle. "So I asked him. I said, 'Dad, why'd you and Mom have eleven kids?'"

"Eleven kids!"

"You know what he said? He said, 'Son, your mom wanted an even dozen, being Catholic and all, but by then I couldn't oblige her anymore.'"

Follet's face turned red. It reminded Boyd of the police-car flashers. The chief rose and pulled on his sports jacket. He mumbled something about an appointment and offered the service of a patrol car.

Boyd declined. He didn't need a patrol car to show him home. Boyd had a client. Boyd Sherman was a sober sonofabitch.

"You know what they say," said Follet. "Sober up a horse thief and what do you got?"

"A sober horse thief," answered Boyd.

Follet winked. "Talk to you tonight."

They shook hands.

"Kimosabe, how come that pretty wife left you anyway?"

"Ice fishing," said Boyd.

Follet thought about that, then nodded. Next he fished in his jacket for a mob of keys and dropped them into the parka. "It's the small one," he said. "Leave 'em on the desk." He opened the door and peeked into the hall like he was making a getaway.

"Chief," said Boyd.

"Yeah?"

Boyd raised the envelope he'd taken from Jennifer's outfit and pointed at the sign. "What's this?" he asked.

Chief closed the door and took the envelope. He studied it for a second while rubbing his nose. "It's a cattle brand. Where'd you get this?"

Boyd snatched it from the chief's grip. "Let's just say I saw it in my sleep."

Follet's face sagged. He stared at his chess partner and sighed wearily. "Watch your step, greenhorn," he said, and left the office.

The crime reports began with the most recent and went back a couple of years. The file marked "Municipal Corral" was near the front. Inside were four pages containing the standard stuff along with statements. A Detective Frampton had found an empty tin of Copenhagen. Attached were photos of tire prints.

Boyd recorded it on the envelope with Mrs. Landrus's number, then shoved the papers back. That was when he noticed the photo. It was a three-by-five glossy and the face was familiar. He rummaged in his memory for bar faces but came up empty. On the back it read "Rusty Landrus."

Next he found Landrus's file and checked the time of disappearance. The police had naturally put Landrus together with the horses. Follet had remarked about questionable business trips to Las Vegas. Also to check membership in various breeder's associations. "See Municipal Corral," it read.

That was all. He'd come full circle with nothing to go on. He flipped back to the report and searched for another name. Someone who knew horses and whose last name wasn't Landrus.

Reported as missing, a dozen horses from Horse Thief Canyon, a corral at the west edge of town. Clyde Paulos, proprietor.

Jennifer's "friend."

Boyd snatched the Landrus photo and slammed the drawer shut. He'd always been suspicious of "friends" of married women.

FOUR

▼▼▼▼▼ BY TEN O'CLOCK BOYD had lost both chess games over the phone to the chief. It didn't seem possible. The fact that in two months he had yet to win a Friday night match staggered the mind. "Look at it this way," joked Follet, "it keeps you out of the bars."

Boyd sat at his desk playing over the last game, determined to finish his cigarette before taking the dog out. When he crushed the pack it sounded like his own breath crackling. One didn't quit smoking in the midst of a divorce, he thought. It was only six months since he'd given up the booze. Already he'd lost the comforts of sex and oblivion. What else did God want?

God the Father, the grand master who played a billion chess games at the same time. Boyd had tried praying since his breakup but still couldn't be sure of divine instructions. There were two clear lines of existence: God and missing Adrian. Right now God called from the bladder of an arthritic Chihuahua.

Outside, the wind cut into Boyd's parka like a pachuco with

a switchblade. He tugged the dog's line and yelled to hurry up. Buck sniffed around on the ice, lifting each paw like it was stung on hot coals.

Boyd unzipped and began to relieve himself when a rack of searchlights mounted on a truck whipped around the lot and bore down on him. In a blast of radio Jennifer climbed down and called her dog. Together, woman and dog looked fierce, like a K-9 drug patrol.

That's when the fight started. The animals dove into each other, making ugly shadows on the snow. Boyd scooped up Buck in his arms and backed into the trailer. "Shut up," he yelled. But the dog wouldn't stop yelping, his bald, white body quivering, his eyes bulging from his skull. Jennifer had come in and made herself at home. "I put Ranger in the bathroom," she said. "Is it okay?"

Finally, Buck's yelping ended in a paroxysm of wheezing. Jennifer reached for him. "Give him to me," she said.

It was only by handing him over that Boyd realized his hands were splashed with urine.

"He gotcha," observed Jennifer.

She tucked the animal inside her coat so that only his head stuck out between the buttons. He licked her hand.

Boyd went outside and buried his hands in the drift. He rubbed them together and sniffed. They still smelled.

Back inside he found his client sitting on his cot. "I put him under the covers," she explained.

Boyd stood in the doorway wringing his hands.

"Sit down," she said, scooting over.

"What about your truck?" he asked.

"He's not jealous."

Then came an explosion from the Y's bathroom. "Your dog is," he said.

"Tell you what," said Jennifer. "Got an extension cord?"

Boyd shrugged.

"I didn't think so. She leaned back and crossed her legs. "I got a problem. The cord to my block heater won't make it inside. Now, If I'm to stay, someone's got to run out every hour and turn the engine over."

"I see," he said, unable to get hold of his voice.

"I got your bike in my truck," she told him. "Thought you'd need it."

"Thanks."

She watched him, then kind of smiled. "Be right back," she said, jumping up.

He watched her enter the YWCA bathroom and slam the door. All at once the barking stopped. When she came out the dog was with her. "This is Ranger," she said.

He was a blue roan with white spots and in the kitchen light had green eyes. "He's a Dingo," she added.

She buttoned her coat. "I'm starved. Tell you what, you call Happy Trails and order and Ranger and me'll pick it up."

When she left he went into the Y's office and made a list. Fifty below zero and she craved wonton. For him, lots of rice. He liked rice. Doloras called it the perfect food, five yin to one yang, harmony, like polygamy. Rice didn't make grease. He hated grease. Bachelorhood was greasy. To be single meant thin and pimply, with filthy sheets. Which reminded him. Straighten up the place. Clean off the desk. Leave the chess set but arrange the pieces in a more daring configuration.

He called the Happy Trails and got Doloras. He told her who it was and she said horse chestnuts. He tried to order but all she said was horse chestnuts. "Horse chestnut share," she said. She didn't know who he was. Maybe it was an aphrodisiac, he thought. "Yes," he agreed, "horse chestnut share." "Okay," she said.

Happy Trails was a place where criminals felt welcome, a place where Christ would have hung out with the hookers. At the counter old waitresses gave you steamy looks while you flipped through Hank Williams on the juke. Doloras the Dragon Lady had tiny tattoos on her hands. Whenever customers asked for change she'd grin, half-toothless, and answer, "Faaan-tastic." Doloras's Happy Trails had become an institution, while the locals tried to figure what exactly she was about. In the yellow pages her ad read, *A Tradition in Medicine Dog Since 1966*.

Boyd liked to go off and sit at the Trails. Everybody knew everybody and the newspapers were free. It was there he decided to try investigating for a living. He'd talked it over with Doloras and she thought it a good idea. She cast the *I Ching* and it said okay. "You meet interesting people," she'd told him.

When Jennifer got back she ran a high-powered cord from her block heater into the office. That made it impossible to shut the front door. This she remedied by pulling up the carpet and gouging out a channel in the floor with her jackknife.

The food was a greasy bag of wonton and a smaller bag of fortune cookies. A half-dozen oolong teabags and containers of Chinese mustard completed the order.

"What's this?" he asked.

"Supper," she said.

She was the first real woman he'd seen up close without a coat in weeks. She wore threadbare jeans and a western shirt undone in the front. Her second layer of skin was all thermal.

He emptied a bowl of snow melt into cups and plugged in the element. "How much do I owe you?" he asked.

"No importa," she said, dripping sweet and sour onto a paper plate. "I'm starved."

It was after her fourth wonton that she spoke. "I *love* wonton," she groaned.

When she finished she slurped her tea. Her lips seemed fuller with a coat of grease. "Got enough for another?" she asked.

He boiled more snow for a second round and lit a cigarette.

"You're not hungry," she said.

He shook his head. He was listening to the wind as it whinnied in the cracks of the place.

"Got any music?" she asked.

"Radio in my office."

"Let's go in there," she said.

They took their tea and cookies into his office and read their fortunes. She sat on the cot and flicked on the radio. Country music, it was all you could get.

"I'm year of the tiger," she announced. "I'm good at keeping ghosts away."

"It's a good night for ghosts," he said, sitting at his desk.

She leaned forward and sipped from her cup. "What can we do about that?" she asked.

"Talk."

"You like to talk."

"It's how I work."

"Stop working," she said.

"What?"

"I'm not paying you to work now."

"Talk about what you like," he said.

"Let's talk about what I have to do to get you over here."

Boyd lit a cigarette. "I'm married."

"Sure you are."

She took his cigarette, stubbed it, then took both his hands. "Listen," she said, "it's been three months, you understand?" She looked up from his hands. "It's a good night for ghosts, remember?"

Together with the wind and the wafer-thin ringing of the radio, her scent arched his senses into a cathedral of middle age. His sudden ambition confused him. He thought of prayer. It wasn't sex so much as a kind of life he wanted. He'd always confused the two. Sex was knee-jerk; it was the way you thought about yourself, not just women. Sex was what you made yourself better with. But his separation had ended all that. It was a night for ghosts, all right.

"It's all right," she said. She turned off the light and undressed. He could see her chilled nipples against the kitchen light. Her scent poured from her like a layer of clothing, sweet and sour filling up the place. "Hurry," she urged, tugging on the army blanket.

The cot wasn't made for two adults and a dog. He put Buck in United Way, then lay on his side watching the shadows of branches move across her face. God sent married women like he sent winter storms, he thought. They were to be avoided.

She curved her body against his and rubbed until, finally warmed, she got on top and shook her hair. She went into a routine, a chain of small maneuvers honed to perfection after five years of marriage. She spoke to his penis, calling it wonton. She tried every move there was but no dice.

"It's been like this for a while," he explained.

"We almost had it," she said.

She lay for a long time, humming to the radio. Every so often she'd squeeze him with her thighs, hard, horse-woman thighs, and she'd sigh on his chest.

When he finally decided to help her, she held his face. "It's all right," she said. "I'll take care of it later."

He lit a cigarette and lay back. She would be asleep soon. He listened to the wind, to the plastic sheeting on the window balloon with each gust. Curled behind him was his first client. Hard to believe. It had even sounded hollow when he told Chief Follet that afternoon. First client. He turned it over in his mind in search of some original meaning. Client was someone for whom you performed a service. Very funny, he thought. You embark on a marvelous journey, said his fortune.

But this was real life, where men went limp and sports heroes took dope. The private-eye thing was sentimental. Like love stories, like the glamour of crime. Like being single. It was enough to make a grown man blush.

There must have been a noise, an involuntary groan, for she got up on her elbows and looked at him. "You okay?" she asked.

"Thirsty," he said.

As Boyd entered the hall, Buck went crazy in United Way, yipping like someone possessed. Then Ranger joined in, telegraphing in the dark. Boyd stood shivering while pouring ice water. Suddenly he broke into a howl. It felt good. He howled some more. "Ah-hooo," he called. Like a wolf.

For a moment the beasts were silent.

FIVE

▼▼▼▼▼ ON SATURDAYS EVERYTHING SHUT down. The offices were closed and the cleaning lady didn't come till Sunday. Saturdays Boyd slept in and dreamt of Phoenix. In some dreams he was drunk. Then he'd wake up and wonder if it was true.

Jennifer shaking him. "Somebody's here," she said.

"What?"

"Somebody's here."

It was Adrian. "Boyd?" she called.

Buck flipped at the sound of her voice. Then Ranger tuned up. Boyd curled up with the blanket and shut his eyes.

When he peeked she was standing in the doorway, the cold rolling off her in tongues. She had Bud, the border collie she'd got from the ranch. Bud was her boy.

"Well-how-do-you-do?" she purred, like she'd drawn a bead on the biggest bull elk this side of Jackson.

Jennifer sat up. "Do I know you?" she asked.

"It's okay," said Adrian. "Believe me."

"Glad you approve," said Jennifer.

"What do you want, Adrian?" he asked.

Adrian needed his signature.

"Just leave it," he said.

"I need it now," she insisted, raising her voice in competition with the dogs. She drew a pen from her vest and offered it. "It's the title to the truck."

He signed it.

"Did you get the papers?" she asked.

"What?"

"The papers!"

"What papers?"

"You know what papers. You got twenty days."

"What?"

Something crashed. First there was a break in the barking followed by the pounding of a beast intent on settling a score. Ranger had busted out. "Look out!" shouted Boyd, battening down the blanket.

Ranger blew in the doorway, up over the cot, and right up the wall. He had Bud by the throat. Jennifer jumped up and began tugging at her dog. "Ranger, dammit," she yelled, banging him on the head. Adrian tried forcing herself between the animals. The dogs gnarled and then squealed while the women shouted instructions. Finally Adrian ran out and came back with a bucket.

"No!" Boyd yelled.

Ice water shattered over them like a pane of glass. Jennifer screamed. Boyd grabbed Bud and dragged him out. Naked, both man and woman stood shivering. When he tried covering her with the wet blanket she threw it at him. "Don't touch me," she said.

Boyd opened the bathroom to get some towels. Buck rushed out chirping like a windup toy before Adrian snatched him up and tossed him in the closet. Boyd came out with a towel around himself. "Anything else?" he asked.

Adrian picked up the truck title and shook off the water. She grinned at Jennifer. "Nice meeting you," she said.

Detective and client dressed in silence. "Bull," Adrian had called him. Bull Sherman. Adrian could really be cruel. Maybe that's why he'd married her. It challenged him to match her word for word, tit for tat, then nail her good in bed. Slam dunk at the buzzer. Put that in your sports page.

But that was over. Bull Sherman had lost his wonton. He remembered what an old-timer had said at an AA meeting once. "Sex ain't a problem when a good shit feels better than a piece of ass."

Things had changed, all right. Now he'd spend his life with women who had holes in their arms.

Strictly business, he reached over and took her arm. "Hey, what the hell?" she said, yanking it back.

"They're fresh," he said.

She turned his radio up loud. He decided not to push it. After all, she was paying him. She was his ticket out of there, away from cowboys, snow, and dumb pickup trucks. For that he'd take shit off anybody.

The Mustang Cafe was quiet but for a high-school kid performing surgery on the *Stampede*. Her sweat shirt read MEDICINE DOG HIGH. When she looked up she had print smeared on her face.

"Keeping a scrapbook?" Boyd asked.

"Kinda."

"Sports?"

She stopped cutting and looked up. "Huh?"

"Just curious," he said.

She resumed chewing gum and blew a huge bubble. When it burst, she inhaled it. "I'm supposed to keep everything about the horse rustling," she explained.

"Keep you busy?"

She snapped her scissors like she was cutting hair. "Kinda," she said.

Enter Clyde Paulos from the kitchen. He was tall and cancer-thin in a western shirt worn snapped to the neck. He had steely gray hair and when he smiled you saw false teeth the color of corpses. Deep snout lines gave him a look of sincerity like an ageless Nashville crooner, the kind that liked kids, shot heroin, and played the Opry.

"Susan, you get back to work."

The kid gathered her scraps and headed through the swinging doors.

Boyd and Jennifer took a table in the back. "Kinda dead here," he said.

Jennifer seemed distracted. "What?" she asked.

Watching his client he felt like a guy who'd just driven all night in a blackout and come to in a diner in Nebraska.

"Dead," he repeated.

"Who?"

"Your husband maybe."

"Rusty? Why do you say that?"

"Because that's what happens."

She ordered the works—eggs, sausage, pancakes, and potatoes. The thought of her husband dead didn't exactly curb her appetite. A junkie with an appetite, that excited him. For women, men were a fact of life; for men, sex was that fact. Men blew in like ghosts, rattling all the shingles and generally raising hell.

"Tell me about him," he said.

There wasn't much to tell. They'd met in Vegas while she was on vacation. He said he was an insurance adjustor. She said she didn't know what that was. The day before she was to return to Iowa, he proposed, offering a large diamond and a life full of horses. He had a friend in Wyoming.

"When did you come to Medicine Dog?"

"Four years ago, after we bought the horses."

First came Zaba, an Arabian. They got him at an auction in Scottsdale, Arizona, just before moving north. Arabians were special, she said. Wyoming was quarter-horse country but she'd match her Zaba against any cow pony. Zaba was her baby.

She and Rusty had joined all the big horse associations and traveled the circuit. Soon she owned a reputation and a half dozen of the finest show horses in town. "They're all gone now," she sighed. "Stolen except for Zaba and Chestnut." Horse Chestnut was Rusty's mare.

"I don't know about horses," said Boyd.

"Neither did Rusty at the beginning," she said.

"Know somebody who'd like to kill him?"

"The police already asked me."

"What did you tell them?"

Suddenly she clammed up. Clyde Paulos had ambled over to a family with two kids. He laughed out loud and mussed the hair of the young boy. The family behaved like he was a priest.

"Go on," said Boyd.

Jennifer had lost her appetite. "Let's go."

"I asked you a question."

"And I answered it," she said testily.

"You didn't kill him, did you? Did you kill him?"

"You're not even funny," she said.

"Mrs. Landrus, why don't you level with me? You hired me to get answers."

"What are you talking about?"

"Pecos over there. Are you working with him or me? Because if it's him, give me my money and I'll pay for breakfast. I don't care if you murdered your husband."

He said that last part loud enough for everyone in the place to hear. Paulos looked over. He stood before the window bathed in light. When he stretched he swelled like a snake. He was coming their way.

Clyde didn't even acknowledge her. "Clyde Paulos," he said, shaking hands. "I know who you are."

"Boyd Sherman. And no you don't."

Paulos's eyes wandered to Jennifer. "Mrs. Landrus, how are you doing?"

Jennifer was buttoning her coat. She nodded.

Paulos answered for her. "Good as can be expected, I imagine."

He stood over them grinning for a few seconds. That's when Boyd noticed the man's belt buckle. The cross and star emblem again. When Paulos resumed speaking it was to Boyd, but his eyes never left Jennifer.

"When it comes to horses, this lady's the best. If there's anything I can do, don't hesitate to call. What I mean, Mr. Sherman, is find Rusty Landrus."

"That's fine," said Boyd. "Now do you mind telling me what Rusty Landrus has to do with you?"

"Beg pardon?"

"Exactly how long have you been attending to his wife?"

Paulos brought his hands to his belt. The yokel lines had gone from his face. "What do you mean?" he asked.

Boyd stood up. "You know what I mean."

Jennifer broke the ice. She jumped up and waved the bill in Clyde's face. "I got to go feed," she said.

Paulos followed them to the door. "Jenny," he said, "you tell Mr. Nice Guy there he'd better stay out of my dining establishment until he apologizes to you."

"I will," she said.

At the corrals they sat in the truck with the engine running. It was just like he'd imagined, only close up it was even starker. It looked like those grainy black-and-white photos of the scene of the crime, any homicide, so long as it was grisly.

The place consisted of rows of tar-paper shacks squared by a series of dirt roads that met at the end and ran another hundred yards to the river. Signs bearing ownership wagged from fence poles. Cats roamed everywhere, fat and crazy-looking, among the pens.

Jennifer was explaining the history of the place. It had once been a ferry crossing on the Overland Trail. "People are buried right under us," she said. The pioneers were down there, sinking or rising like the river, seeking repose under all that horseshit.

"What did Paulos tell you?" he interrupted.

She said that he'd called her and said not to hire a private investigator. He'd told her to call it off.

"You mean you didn't tell him about me?"

"Why should I?"

That's what he liked about Jennifer—her loyalty.

So Clyde Paulos was that "friend in Wyoming" she'd spoken about. Clyde knew Rusty from before, she said. Illinois, in fact. Rusty was an insurance man in Cicero and traveled a lot. Clyde was one of his better-informed clients. They'd kept in touch after Clyde retired to Medicine Dog. He had family here. The Pauloses had owned the Mustang for fifty years and knew everybody. Clyde spent much of his time on the rodeo circuit sending back enlarged glossies of himself bull riding, which his brother hung in the cafe.

Five years ago he'd retired from competition after breaking his pelvis and decided to put his savings into horses. He bought Horse Thief Canyon at the edge of town and renovated the stables. He supplied rodeo stock to the intermountain region and had a reputation for putting on a good show. "Get good stock and good clowns," she said. "That's the secret."

Two years ago, after running uncontested for a city council seat, he informed Chief Follet, "You're dead meat."

"Is that why you're afraid of him?" asked Boyd.

"I ain't afraid of him."

"Then tell me something." He unfolded the envelope addressed to Paulos and pointed to the cattle brand. "What's this mean?"

She studied it for a second. "Where'd you get that?" she asked.

Boyd pointed to the dash. "Right there."

She felt around on the dash and sighed. "You oughtn't to snoop around in people's things," she snapped.

"So what is it?"

She glanced at the envelope again. "That?" she said. "Everyone knows what that is. That's North Star brand."

Boyd folded the envelope and tucked it inside his coat. "Where's that?"

"I don't know," she said. "Up north, I reckon."

In the gloom of the stable stood a magnificent animal wearing a blanket. Its coat was so thick you could bury your hands in it. When they entered, it snorted.

"Zaba," purred Jennifer, stroking its neck. Finally she turned to Boyd. "Put out that cigarette," she ordered.

When he came back inside he found her feeding. "He's my gray," she announced.

As he watched them he realized he didn't trust women or horses. Putting the two together only made it worse. Beauty and the beast. He felt left out.

After finishing with the gelding they went next door. "This is Horse Chestnut," she said. The Quarter Horse looked like a warm fur coat. "Notice the eyes, they're blue. That's called 'glass-eyed.' She's a bald-face, glass-eyed chestnut. That's rare."

The horse laid its ears back and watched him. There was

something spooky about those eyes, all right. Milky, like an albino's, but weirder.

"She's got a baby in the barn," said Jennifer.

He looked around. "Where?"

"That means she's with foal. You sure don't know much about horses," she observed.

Outside were four mustangs in a separate corral, all bunched together against the wind, their fur riffling. "They're still wild," she said. "People just buy 'em and forget 'em. People don't care. Some don't even feed their horses. You see 'em in the spring with their ribs sticking out. It's criminal and the law just sits on its ass. Jesus, I hate people."

SIX

▼▼▼▼▼ THAT NIGHT BOYD ATTENDED a Medicine Dog High home game. The Mustangs were hopeless. It wasn't enough to get the game over the radio. You had to be there. Some guy called himself coach, the kind of guy who taught a cretinous brand of Social Studies and attended union meetings.

Never mind. Adrian was there.

He spotted her halfway up the opposite side of the gym. They were playing the national anthem. His hand was over his heart.

He was certain she was staring at him. Naw, he thought. Adrian was not the kind of woman who pretended not to see you. Adrian, when she attended a basketball game, by God, watched basketball.

She wore the school's green sweater and sat alone with her knees together sipping Coke through a straw. Adrian, alone on weekends. Adrian humming to herself in the apartment, Adrian watching TV, eating frozen dinners, watching the wall. It was gut-wrenching to imagine. He was gripped by the urge to run over and gobble her up in his arms. You poor lonely person, I love you, he'd say. I've loved you from the bleachers for centuries, lifetimes, aeons of interstellar yearning!

After the game he rode his bike home, undressed, and lay in bed talking to God. He said to bless the girl in the green sweater. He'd made such a mess of things and he was tired. Then he fell asleep.

Later he dreamed about Jennifer and Rusty. "Oh Rusty," she said, "please don't hate me."

Rusty sulking at the kitchen table, straight whiskey in the glass. In one of his dark moods. "Shut up, Jen. Shut up, Jen, I'm warnin' ya."

Strictly small change. Did she love him? Strike that. Why'd she stay with him? And why hire a private investigator to find the sonofabitch?

The first question was easy. People stayed: simple. They stayed even when their hearts and minds had gone and there was nothing but TV and leftover chicken. They stayed because there was no mercy, period.

The second question would require digging. Insurance, maybe. Maybe just to prove something to the cops, to Clyde Paulos, to herself.

His watch said five when the phone rang. At five A.M. either somebody'd died or wanted a big favor.

"Hello."

"They stole my horses," she said.

"Say that again."

"The bastards stole my horses. What are we going to do?"

Horses again. The country had begun its long slide from third base into the twenty-first century, and folks were stealing horses. Horses weren't sports cars you took to the moon. Horses belonged to knotty old men who believed all that shit on "Gunsmoke" twenty-five years ago. Dammit, horses weren't mainstream.

"Have you called the cops?"

"No."

"Well, don't. Where are you?"

"At home."

"Stay put until you hear from me. Give me time to look around."

"I can't believe this is happening," she said. "They'll hurt them, I just know it. How can anyone hate horses?"

"I don't know."

"They're perverted," she continued.

"Look," he said, "try and calm down. I'll be in touch."

He hung up. Mr. Nice Guy, he thought.

He got up and turned on the light. He fumbled through his desk until he found it. The police photo was the guy, all right. But the name wasn't Landrus.

Jennifer, meet Mr. X.

The door was frozen. He chipped at the hinges but it was no go. The place was sealed. Call Adrian.

"This better be good," she said.

"I need help."

"Boyd? What's wrong?"

"I'm stuck at my place. The door's frozen and I got an appointment."

There was a pause in which he imagined her covering the receiver to inform Jack of the situation. Jack, large and hairy and groggy after a bad night of war flashbacks.

"What do you want me to do?" she asked.

"Torch me out."

"Give me ten minutes."

She hung up.

He sat at the kitchen table staring at the envelope from Jennifer's outfit. "Man see horse," he wrote. He'd seen it in Chinese on the Happy Trails menu. Doloras had translated. For answers he'd have to leave town. He'd always craved traveling. Now he was getting paid to.

He sat in a chair with a blanket while Adrian went over the door with the torch. By the time he'd boiled water she'd thawed out the lock and was banging the door with her weight. Finally it popped. "There," she announced, out of breath.

"Come in," he said.

"Did you sign those papers?"

She said she was in a hurry. She unzipped her parka and leaned against the refrigerator with a cup of coffee. "Saw your girlfriend," she said.

"She's a client," he corrected.

"Whatever you call her, she's sure in a hurry."

"When did you see her?"

"Just now. Doing seventy up Utah."

"Are you sure?"

"Blonde in a Ford pickup with that dog?"

Boyd grunted into his cup.

"She's trouble for you," said Adrian.

"You think so?"

She watched him for a second, then drained her cup. "Gotta go," she announced.

He watched her tug on her mittens. Then he remembered: the corrals. "Can I get a ride?" he asked.

Her hand dropped from the doorknob. Dramatic. She got that way when she knew it was useless. "I'm in a hurry, Boyd."

"Just be a second," he said, going to his office for his coat.

"Dammit, Boyd! I don't appreciate this."

"It's business."

When he got into the truck she was watching the moon fade in the west. Across the street two Union Pacific diesels played chicken in the switching yard. The street was empty.

"Okay, tell me where we're going."

"Phoenix."

"I'm not in the mood."

"Just head west on eighty till Salt Lake, then hang a left," he said. "It's easy."

"Boyd, cut it out."

"Cut what out?"

"You know what I mean. Cut it out or get out of my truck."

"*My truck*, she says. When did it become *my truck*?"

"You need a ride or not?"

"Corrals," he said. "Take me there." Then he was shouting. "What's so important you're late for anyhow?"

She drove in silence. Finally he had to say it. "Who's keeping your bed warm for you?"

That did it. The truck slid to a stop in the middle of the bridge. "Get out," she ordered.

"Come on," he said.

She reached for the glove compartment and withdrew a .22 revolver. "Flake off, mister."

"Where the hell you get that? Okay," he said, putting up his hands. "Just answer me something."

"Move!"

He slammed the door. As she drove off he packed a snowball and whipped it at the truck. It disintegrated into powder.

The clock on the Rocky Mountain Savings & Loan read minus fifty-eight. It was a little after six. He looked up into the pale rocks that encircled the town and shivered. He tied his hood and headed for the temperature sign. That was Bridger. Turn left and your back was to the wind. Two blocks and you're there. Scene of the crime.

He stood for a long time in the corner of the stable. He had become a horse. Or rather he occupied the mare's thoughts of herself at home. As Boyd became conscious of himself, the horse and the horse's memory of a man smelling of tobacco came into Boyd's mind. That was horse vision. Horse sense was not rudimentary common sense at all. Horse sense was refracted, sliced by angles of light, mystical. Horses lived the epistemology of biblical manna, their ears cocked and heads shaking.

Horses were wealth, the idea of horses, the great herds. They had always lived, rumbling east to west and back. Wind people, Wind River, horses and names the color of manure. Horseshit, manna, food of the gods.

Then like a horse he sensed disturbance, something about the light as it spread over the snow, something not earth.

It was a personalized tin of chewing tobacco, DWL embossed like a cattle brand on the lid. He remembered the crime report in Follet's office. A Lieutenant Frampton had found a tin of snouse. He dipped into it and sniffed. Kosher it wasn't. He took a pinch and lodged it in his cheek. Food of the gods.

Right then something didn't want him to leave, something close. Someone was calling. Nice guy, it said. Hey, Mister Nice Guy, drawled like a threat. Hey, it whispered.

By then he'd made it the length of the stables and stood among the debris. Ancient horse trailers and lumber strewn everywhere. Horse people's droppings, like the bodies of pioneers. Again, manna.

Hey, Nice Guy.

Beyond the trash lay the river. From the bank he could see the railroad on the other side, the downtown and interstate carved out of the rock. The river whispered. A blank sheet, it stretched less than a football field to the other bank. Small black birds swooped over the ice while somewhere a magpie screeched.

He stepped onto the ice and heard it crunch. For a second he didn't feel cold. His father was close now, squatting out there, looking off at nothing. He'd be talking about the cold, how you didn't think about it. Warmth was just not thinking about it.

The moment he saw the fishing hole he knew. He knew ice. Ice was a church he'd grown up in, fished in, heard in his sleep. He could judge thickness by color, by the purr of footstep.

It was the body, its face bloated, eyes milky like those of the mare, but strangely alert, like he saw something monstrous in the sky.

Jennifer, meet Rusty.

SEVEN

▼▼▼▼▼ LANDRUS, AKA CUBIT, first name Maxwell. At least that was what he was when he bought drinks at the Starlighter in Phoenix a few years back. Boyd recalled getting drunk and discussing the ontology of air conditioning with him. Cubit had looked exactly then as he did on ice, bloated and spooked. He shook out his shoulder-length red hair and said, "I'm going to Vegas. I know some people there." He wore an open silk shirt with a gold chain, drank gin, and smoked Kools. "Call me Max."

Max Cubit, a man on his way to becoming Rusty Landrus. That was what guys like Max did in Vegas. Maybe that was why so many borderline types came to the desert. They changed names like snake skin and drove fast cars in a straight line until the engine gave out or they wrecked. Lawyers representing wives sniffed around old bars trying to collect money. That was where Boyd first got the idea of becoming a private eye. The image had roared out of the desert like an American Book of Revelation, like truck drivers and rock bands.

He remembered Max Cubit, all right. Cubit the henchman

who'd inspired him to try the business. You didn't need to be a pro to sense that here was a man in trouble, cheap trouble that men wearing pimp clothes and cologne got into. Bad checks and low-rent hustles, a little dope. Gun without a permit. The topless barmaid called him Red. He spoke fast and never looked you in the eye until late when he got as cold as Swedish sex. It passed for honesty, Viet-vet sweaty nightmare honesty. He'd lean over the table and squint. "Mr. Nice Guy," he snarled. "Am I right?"

He'd done two tours in 'Nam with Special Forces. MOS, long-range assassin. He'd already left his body. "I'm CIA," he said.

Seeing as Mr. Cubit had just bought another round . . . CIA, of course. If Cubit wanted to be a cowboy, then Boyd would be a cowboy. Truck driver, Marine, ditto.

"You think I'm shittin' ya?"

Boyd shook his head. He explained that he saw no reason why the man should be shitting him.

Cubit launched into his resumé.

The great thing about psychopaths was that truth or fiction, it didn't matter. Guys like Cubit lived their stories, even if it was only inside their heads. They persisted in pinning everything on a few large themes. Boyd knew the layout of the land. His own story was about a brilliant young sports writer who traveled, siring kids and ducking out on marriages. Highways, motels, all-night TV. The thing about guys like Cubit was that they thought they never hurt anyone.

"So where was I?" slurred Cubit.

"Cicero."

"Yeah, so there's this accident. It wasn't my fault. This guy I'm working with, it was him."

"What kind of accident?"

"Serious, believe me. At least Manetti thought so."

"Manetti?"

"He's big," said Cubit. "Never mind."

"Is Manetti CIA?"

Cubit shook some ice into his mouth and slammed down the glass. "CIA? Jesus Christ, this ain't CIA, this is the Organization."

Boyd lit the man's cigarette.

"Organization," barked Cubit, like he was teaching a dog a new command. "The Mob. Whaddya think we're talking here?"

Cubit ordered more drinks, then went to the men's room. The barmaid crossed the pile carpeting, scraping up sheet lightning with her spiked heels. She had breasts right out of French Impressionism. Boyd gave her quarters. "Play something nice," he said.

Flesh was water-cooled, like air conditioning, he thought, feeling his brain cells pop with the soaking of alcohol. It reminded him of those packaging pimples they wrapped stereos in. He loved to sit in the apartment and pop one at a time, whole sheets of the things like machine gun belts of nipples.

Music, alcohol, and air conditioning, a rearrangement of molecules, light to darkness, water to ice, an embalming. Everything was going to be okay, he thought. He still had his looks and he was the best writer on the paper except for McLaren. Boyd lit his next cigarette, a man in control.

Cubit got back and slammed his drink, then ordered two more. V for victory, V for peace.

"On the house," said the barmaid.

"See you after work?" asked Cubit.

"Can't," she said. "Got to baby-sit."

"Baby-sit," snorted Max. "Nobody has babies anymore. Least nobody white."

When she turned tail, Max winked. "She likes you," he said. "Believe me, I can tell."

Boyd smirked and studied his drink.

"You think I'm shittin'."

Boyd didn't believe that in the course of normal events that remark deserved a reply.

"I'm talking to you," snapped Cubit. "You think I'm shittin' you or what?"

Boyd puffed his cheeks and exhaled. Like a bullet it struck him why the hell was he sharing his booth, his afternoon, in fact his brief, tentative life with this moron? He never used to drink in dives like the Starlighter. Strictly used car, a step above bowling alleys.

"*No*," said Boyd, aiming his finger right at the man's face. "*You are not shitting. You are a fire-eater, you are a beautiful human being.*"

God help me, he thought, and I'll never drink again.

"You're crazy," said Cubit. "Mr. Nice Guy Crazy Fucker. You're all right."

That's when he let go about his connection with the Syndicate. He'd been hired to do a job in Illinois for an insurance adjustor. It involved a small-businessman in Cicero who'd gotten out of line. Nothing serious. But there was a screw-up and somebody'd got killed.

"That's what I thought I was hired for," said Cubit.

It was the wrong someone.

"Hell, I thought the war was over. It's just like 'Nam."

He was getting weepy. The barmaid brought more drinks and touched his shoulder. "It's okay, Red," she said.

"I'm cool," he said.

Sure, you're cool, thought Boyd. Emotional cues right out of TV. Savages, that's what we were. Children dressed up like Barbie dolls, color-coordinated. Americans didn't need TV, they lived it. We're all cool, he thought.

Boyd had come to the Starlighter state of existence because there he actually appeared sane. Just visiting, he thought. Which was true. Before the year was up he took a two-week vacation to drink in the park. He said he needed sun.

McLaren would shake his head. Fast gun McLaren. The bastard actually fired six-shooters on weekends. Tin cans at the ranch. From horseback he'd shoot rattlers. He hated rattlesnakes. Drunk one night he shot the stack off a kerosene lamp. "This gun," he said, "belonged to Buffalo Bill Cody. Got it from a publisher in Salt Lake."

Boyd understood that the western mystique was the care and maintenance of equipment. The old lore pivoted on excellence, hand-hewn and polished with the oil of a man's hand. He recalled once seeing the typewriter that had belonged to Mark Twain. He just knew that on that machine he could punch out a story oozing black mud, that would blow out over the fairways cawing like an embittered crow. That's what drew him to Wyoming. The hardness, the hard, straight lines of seeing, of fenceposts, of false teeth in the cups of pioneers.

Max Cubit had become an enforcer, a technician who could snuff out opposition on the big board. He partook of the legend and it ate him up. Big grin and a silencer: Max Cubit, company man. The hitch was that after the last job he'd jumped companies. Somebody had whispered back in Cicero. With his tune played out, Cubit took an all-expense-paid vacation at the request of the Feds. Six months in a vets hospital followed by a transfer. Phoenix was just a stop on his way to meet his assignment in Vegas. He knew how things worked there, he said.

Now he lay face up in a foot of ice. Something had happened in Vegas, all right. Who was to say he wouldn't some day be cataloged in western annals as a hero, like Butch Cassidy in Bolivia. Gory, gruesome death like legends of sex feats hung like sunset behind the pecking of the tabloids. Twain understood that. He saw Americans condemned to impersonate what they feared. In church, clergy spoke of the blood of the lamb. Las Vegas was the new stockyard.

Ciao, Rusty.

. . .

"Mrs. Landrus, your husband's dead. Am I still working for you or not?"

He'd rehearsed it several times before calling her.

It wasn't until noon when she arrived at the river that she answered his question. Cops were all over the place. A jackhammer stuttered out on the ice.

"You okay?" he asked.

She had to think about it.

He climbed in her husband's pickup beside her and dipped some chew. It was the tin from the corral. The sight of it sure tightened her straps. She got right to the point.

"What makes you think my husband was murdered?" she asked.

"Mrs. Landrus, this may be hard to believe but I met your husband in Phoenix. He seemed in a lot of trouble. He struck me as being a lot of things but a suicide wasn't one of them."

"I know," she said. "He'd told me about you."

"What did he say?"

"That you're honest. My husband needed a friend."

"What for?"

She looked out the window. "It doesn't matter. He's dead."

"Mrs. Landrus, am I working for you or not?"

She glanced at him and nodded.

"Then it matters," he said.

"You think I'm lying, don't you? You think I killed my husband."

She buried her head in his chest and he held her that way.

"It's Clyde, isn't it?" she said.

"I don't like him," he said.

"Why?"

"I don't like him. You analyze it."

Chief Follet appeared on the bank, hunkered over like a brave doing some deep, earth-felt stomp to the beat of his bear heart. Approaching the pickup he beat himself with his arms for warmth.

Chief motioned for her to roll down her window. Instead she opened the door. "Mrs. Landrus," he said, "I'm sorry it's under these circumstances that we have to meet again. It might be awhile. You're welcome to stay or go home and we'll call you for identification."

"I'll stay," she said.

Follet looked at Boyd. "Can I see you a moment?"

Boyd watched him trudge back to the river. Jennifer turned off the ignition and both detective and client sat in silence, watching the windows steam up. "Answer me something," he said, holding up the tobacco tin. "Who's DWL?"

She glanced at it, then at him. "Where'd you find that?"

"In your stable this morning. Who is he?"

"She was staring out the window. "Ling," she said.

"First name?"

"D. W.—I don't know."

He wrote it on the envelope. "D. W. Ling. What's that—Chinese?"

She nodded.

"Did Rusty know him?"

"No," she replied.

"That sounds definite."

Rusty had known about him, she explained, but had never met him. "He didn't know about Clyde's relationship to him."

"Which was?"

"Horses."

When Boyd caught up with Follet the jackhammer resumed and he had to shout. "Find anything?" he asked.

"Fresh prints, western heel," said Follet. "Figure two men, medium build. They're headed for Utah."

"How you figure?"

"Ever hear of the Outlaw Trail? Remind me to tell you about it sometime."

"The crime report said north," said Boyd.

"It's the same trail. In the old days it went to Mexico. Now it's a network of some pretty sophisticated crooks."

Just then the acetylene torch came on. "Looks like you got a stuck one," said Boyd.

"Huh?"

"Landrus."

"You mean Cubit, don't you?" Follet was staring at him. "Yeah, he's stuck, but he'll come loose. What about you?"

The two men went out on the ice. The men respected Follet. He was easygoing and knew lots of jokes. But they knew one thing, that Chief Follet had seen more ammo fired in anger than they had on the range. In LA he'd done everything. In this town he was John Wayne.

Follet had taken command of the various city departments out on the ice, and if the mayor had a problem with that, he said, she could come down here herself and supervise. He was on the radio to city hall when he turned to Boyd. "They hate my guts," he said.

"It's their show," Boyd replied.

"Until something goes wrong," said Follet. "It's the department's red behind out here, not Mayor Sally's."

Mayor Sally was Sally Crab. A math PhD from Georgia, she'd landed in town during the boom and worked as a stripper from Medicine Dog to Evanston. According to Follet it wasn't until a year ago that her husband and two sons showed up. The family reunited, they bought a home in the fat part of town and settled down.

Sally's first political success was organizing the Newcomers Club. The Newcomers was a band of women who got rowdy on weekends when a male strip show came to town.

Next Sally ran for city council when a seat was vacated suddenly by Josh Twomey who'd contracted cancer of the rectum. The rest was history. Two years later the incumbent mayor stepped down for reasons of "conflict of interest" involving natural gas holdings.

In October a special meeting of the council had been called to discuss the issue of mayor. October was hunting season. In the chambers that night they'd barely gotten a quorum, and of the few present, nobody wanted the job. Nobody but Sally Crab.

"The secret of my success," she often said, "is I surround myself with competent men."

In November, as the first woman mayor in Clearwater County, she bought computers for every department. Of course she had to give up stripping. Too bad, thought some. "She's a better stripper than a mayor," said Follet. "Of course that's hearsay." Then he thought about it for a second. "Even so, a woman's got to think of her future."

By late afternoon Boyd's client had gone and come back and the cops had changed shifts. The news team from WIND radio set up a remote on the bank. Gentleman Mike Hagar, broadcasting from a Dodge van, played music and gave Rusty Landrus updates.

Follet checked his watch and turned to Boyd. "The Superbowl started a half-hour ago," he said. "Go check Hagar for the score, will you?"

Mike Hagar was a small, intense man with a handlebar mustache and a turquoise belt buckle. He sat in a velvet swivel chair at the back of the van wearing a rack of headphones. "Come in," he said in his even baritone.

"Mike Hagar," said the DJ, offering a firm hand.

"Boyd Sherman, private investigator."

Hagar grinned and held up his hands. "I'm clean, I'm mainstream. What do you want to know?"

"Chief wants to know the score of the game."

Hagar's grin spread across his chops and broke into downright disdain. "The chief wants to know the score, does he? Tell him his money's safe. No score after one."

Boyd turned to go.

"Hey," said Hagar, "now it's my turn. Who's the blonde?"

"My client."

"Be a good buddy. Introduce me."

"Introduce yourself," he said.

It wasn't till after eight when they chipped the body free. It took six men to lift it from the river and set it in a body bag. Suddenly released into the air, Rusty Landrus was no longer recognizable. It wasn't until they turned his head that they saw it. The entire back of the skull had been blown away, leaving a picture-window view of his brains.

"High-caliber rifle?" asked Boyd.

"Handgun, point-blank," said Follet. "See the entrance right here? He pointed to a brown hole in the throat. He was in a hurry. "Ask Mrs. Landrus to come down here," he ordered.

Boyd motioned to her but she didn't move. She remained staring down over the bank like a girl on a high board staring into the throat of her first dive. When they lugged the body up on the bank, she froze up. Boyd tried taking her to the truck but it was no use.

"If she can't do this . . ." said Follet.

"Thanks," said Boyd. "I'll take her home."

"Fine with me," said Follet, anxious to get going. He was heading for the van to get the score.

EIGHT

▼▼▼▼ ON THE MORNING OF the funeral the sky was cloudy and the wind sluggish. Boyd sat smoking in Adrian's pickup, the last in a line of six that trailed the hearse up Utah to the cemetery. He was reading Rusty Landrus's obit in the *Stampede*. Adrian was complaining about how long it took to drive a lousy few blocks, and why couldn't he have ridden with his client in the first place?

"Where is she anyway?"

"Who?"

"Miss Jennifer."

"With Pecos."

She sighed through her teeth. "Why the hell don't you get a real job like everyone else and buy a car?" she said.

He banged the paper with the back of his hand. In the "People" section the Chinese community was preparing for its New Year's gala. Featured was a dragon dance and dinner at the Happy Trails. Year of the Horse, announced Don Wei Ling, businessman.

All week he'd tried getting hold of Mr. Ling. "Mr. Ling

busy," said his daughter-in-law. Mr. Ling's son sold Fords in town. "Don't push the river," said the ad for new Broncos. Signed, Al Ling, the Chinaman.

Old man Ling, Mandarin proprietor of Westward Ho Taxidermy and Rancho Bowl, remained active in civic affairs. Just the year before he'd led a voter registration drive. When a Chinese national arrived in town, contact D. W. Ling. "He fix you good," said Doloras at the Happy Trails.

At the cemetery, members of the cortege parked and strolled to the grave with their dogs. In a clearing they stood in a clump, the city workers off to the side, having just dug the grave. The service had been postponed weeks because the ground was frozen solid and the grave warmer hadn't worked. They ended up having to truck one in from Salt Lake City.

Jennifer sat in a folding chair holding a rose. The minister's prayer droned among the pines. The surrounding markers read like the starting five in American history. Eighteen sixty-eight was Promontory; '76, Little Big Horn; '98, Butch Cassidy, along with railroad guys and frozen ranchers; that winter of '88, a schoolteacher. The Chinese were buried everywhere, said Adrian, but no one knew where exactly.

Clyde Paulos stared into the grave. In front of him, Jennifer sat stoically. Next to them, Al Ling, the Ford dealer. The others were just men in suits who appeared at critical moments in everyone's life.

When the prayer ended, the preacher glanced at his watch, then whispered to Jennifer. She stood and set the rose on the casket. That's when the camera flashed. All at once several men took off down the road at a trot. Paulos led the widow to the hearse where a young Chinese guy opened and slammed doors. Within seconds the motorcade passed out of sight down the hill.

The only ones left were the minister and a woman Boyd recognized as the creature who'd served him his divorce papers.

She stood in a fur coat and black dress like a painting, purse in hand and staring out over the town. Her gray-black hair was combed straight back and her eyes were just slits. Here was a hard woman.

The preacher stood by the grave shuffling papers he'd taken from his pocket. When he seemed satisfied with everything, he picked up the rose Jennifer had set on the coffin, sniffed it, and put it in his lapel.

"Howdy," he said.

The preacher chewed tobacco. He took a pinch of Boyd's and waved to the woman. "Go on ahead," he shouted. "I'll be right along."

Then, turning to Boyd, he grinned. "That's my sister," he said. "Salt of the earth." He next offered Boyd his hand. "I'm Abe Marsh," he said. Then his jaw fell and he spat like it was sin. "What the hell?"

"It's Ling's," said Boyd.

"Sheep dip," said the preacher. "Here, try this."

"No, thanks."

Abe Marsh's church was a renovated gas station, an old Citgo with the crank pumps and mechanics' trenches in the garage, built to service the cross-country traffic when the Lincoln Highway was completed in '39. Preacher Marsh had landed here after the war and worked oil rigs for a while. This was his fourth church.

"You know," he said, "in the old days you didn't have these grave warmers. You had to keep the body on ice till spring. Of course if you were moving you had a problem. I heard tell that prospectors up toward Atlantic City would cut the head of the deceased into a point with an ax and drive the sombitch into the ground like a spike.

"You a friend of the deceased?" he asked.

"Friend of his wife," said Boyd.

The fat man's mouth went slack for a moment. "Oh?"

"I was hired to investigate the circumstances surrounding her husband's death."

"Oh, I see."

"Like murder."

Preacher Marsh shook his head. "Who'd get mixed up with something like that?"

"Who'd hire a fat bag of wind like you when there's a real church in town?"

"There's no call to get insulting," said Marsh.

Adrian began leaning on the horn. She flashed her headlights. Boyd grabbed Marsh by the lapels. "You tell Ling I want an interview," he said. "You tell him I got something of his."

"You wouldn't hit a preacher," said Marsh.

Boyd plucked the rose from Marsh's lapel and stuck it in his pocket. "I'm Catholic."

Back in the truck, he was shaking. "Bull's-eye," he said. "I bet I get in to see the old fart in the flesh, what do you want to bet?"

Adrian held out her hand. "Gimme some of that."

She took a pinch of snuff and lodged it in her mouth like a pro. She did things like a pro. He'd married her because she was a lot like a man and it made him feel manly to drive her truck.

"Who took the picture back there?" he asked.

"Cops."

"Oh yeah?"

"Of course. When's the last time they got so many crooks to pose? That funeral was a who's who of the local lodge. Clyde P., Al Ling, the kid who drove the limo . . ."

"And Jennifer Landrus?"

"Now what do you think?"

Boyd surveyed the town from the overpass and laughed.

He'd really gotten himself into a brown bag of shit this time, he thought.

Adrian suddenly flung open the door and leaned out. The truck was doing thirty-five and she had her head hanging out like she was searching the road for loose change. She spat, came up and checked the road, cleared her throat like a coal miner, and spat again.

"Jesus, Boyd," she said, "there's something in that chew besides tobacco."

She spat again, slammed the door, and checked the rearview.

"You ran a red light," he said.

"I don't believe it," she said. "You're dumb. Jesus, you're dumb."

"Where you going?" he demanded.

"We're being tailed."

"What?"

"Don't look now, Mr. Private Eye."

"Who is it?" he demanded.

"How the hell should I know?"

It was a Chevy Suburban blanketed in mud. The windshield was so caked Boyd couldn't see the driver. "Step on it," he said.

"Shut up," she warned.

"That's it," he said, throwing up his hands. "Pull over and drop me off. Did you hear me?"

Heading south at seventy, she ran another light, braked hard, and screeched right at the post office. The truck shot out of a drainage culvert, raced across the Safeway lot, and did a complete U-ey in a grade-school ball field.

"Stop!" he yelled.

There was the yelp of tires and the thump of the truck bed banging the ditch. Snow exploded on the windshield. She flicked on the wipers and downshifted. The wheels spun, heaving geysers of snow into the air. Suddenly the tires grabbed and the truck lunged.

"Turn here," he ordered.

But she didn't. Adrian didn't listen in emergencies. She never listened.

They were out of town doing eighty on a railroad bed beside the river. Instead of music there was the roar of gravel underneath. Adrian squeezed the wheel; one jolt and they'd hit the ties, and at that speed it would flip them into Carbon County. "Take a look," she said.

He figured the Suburban to be about two hundred yards off. No problem, he thought. The Suburban couldn't take as much punishment as Adrian's truck.

"Hold on," she said.

He thought they were rolling. His shoulder banged off the dash and he slid to the floor. The entire outfit shuddered like a nervous breakdown. Adrian had punched the machine over the tracks and taken off toward the rocks. She could lose anybody in the rocks. Just like the rustlers who'd used them for a hundred years to drop out of sight, Adrian knew the rocks.

"Horseshoe Rock," she announced like a cabbie stopping the meter.

Boyd sat for a moment squinting at the top. Clouds rolled low overhead like time-lapse photography, and just above the rock, were two golden eagles. This was the place, he thought. Drop site of the gods. The kind of place you'd stash a thousand pounds of narcotics. The rock had gotten its name from its shape, which could only be viewed from the air. And that was before airplanes.

"I'm going up there," he said.

It required more than a half-hour to climb the rock. Its slickness made footing difficult. Sagebrush and cat's-claw gnarled in the wind. Finally, gasping for breath, he called for help. "I gotta stop," he said.

"At the top," she insisted.

"I'm gonna have a heart attack," he gasped.

Soon they were on the rockface. Sandstone mostly, and higher up, shale. Shale flaked in his hands and cut. Who could live here? he raged. He imagined the men who'd come before, cracked, squirrelly men, mountain men, junior-league capitalists. Even the Indians didn't live here.

"Adrian, help me."

She stood at the summit with her hair fanned out under her stocking cap and waving in the wind. She was a warrior, all right.

He arrived blowing like a thoroughbred. He collapsed on the ground with his head between his knees. When he looked up he could see Ling heading back and the town stretched along the base of the rocks, the river winding through it and the railroad tracks. To the north, the plateau ran for a hundred miles like a flyway.

"What are those?" he asked, pointing to the distant white peaks.

"The Wind Rivers," she replied. "The Indians called them the Shining Mountains."

Indians again.

NINE

▼▼▼▼ WINTER HAD KEPT ITS death hold on Wyoming for so long that spring finally came ferocious and overnight. The wild horses rumbled over the desert in large bands. From the road they resembled not saddle horses so much as buffalo running out from under their winter coats. The mares dropped their foals and the grazing was good. In May the rivers overflowed and the high plains smelled of sage.

On the horizon loomed the Wind Rivers, snow-thick and seething with clouds. Here was the Great Divide, the techtonic thrust separating the Colorado, Columbia, and Missouri. Here began the trees and the ghosts of old mineral rushes, the headwaters of the Green, the caves and sink holes with only Indian names. Wind River, said the map in loose, disjointed letters, suggesting a gathering of sticks, burn-tipped with ancient concerns.

Boyd tossed in his sleep. When he woke, Ranger was sniffing in his ear. In the dull gray light the aspens looked like Chinese courtesans. It was freezing, bone-cold with no place to hide. In cities they were playing baseball, he thought.

Cold had always been his nightmare—cold, moonlight, and the battle of the trees. He'd first seen it in Wisconsin. He was thirteen and confined to bed with the flu. That first night his fever spiked at a hundred four and he saw the trees fighting. It started with the shadows of the branches waving on his closet door. Suddenly the stable character of trees, the distinction between animal and vegetable, became blurred, streaked with lightning and curses.

That was his initiation into manhood, his mountaintop vision. But instead of cementing him to the tribe, it isolated him. His was the secret prize buried at the bottom of the cereal box. *Life was terrifying*.

A month later he experienced his first ejaculation. Lightning and semen. Some kinds of beauty could only exist at low temperatures. God and the broken glass of galaxies. He felt hypnotized as if by oncoming headlights. He steered his life right for it. Wives and lovers had taken turns struggling for control of the wheel, and each had bailed out. Alone he waited for sudden impact, an ejaculation, the ice god.

Nobody but he was crazy enough to spend the night up here. The Shoshones had wintered here only to escape the wrath of the plains tribes. It was the difference between mortal devastation and extinction. Jennifer had told him that.

He wondered about anything Jennifer told him. Why they'd come here, for instance. Why Boyd Sherman, sports fan, lay curled up beneath a Ford pickup with a dog that smelled like crushed pigeons. He could just as easily have been playing the slots at a truckstop in Nevada, or clocking his old MG between Phoenix and LA. He was gambling on something breaking. With Jennifer, things usually happened.

They'd been out barely twenty-four hours and he wasn't sure what she was up to. "To scout horses," she'd said, looking all giddy-up. They were tracking a truck called North Star. Just yesterday he'd seen it in Farson, a crossroads bar and grill midway to the mountains.

It was hauling horses and had pulled in for gas. Boyd couldn't see the stock because of the canvas lashed to the grating. But he could hear them, all right. They were packed tight.

"You a fan of horseflesh?" asked the driver, a big guy with squinty blue eyes and a mustache. Marlboro man.

Boyd set his boot on the rear tire and shrugged. "Kinda," he said.

"There's enough horse in there to feed a kennel of huskies for a year," said Marlboro. "Nothing special."

"Mind if I take a look?"

The man pawed his mustache thoughtfully. "Can't do," he replied. "Federal regulations."

"You mean North Star regulations," said Boyd.

Marlboro grinned. "Same thing," he said. "Now if you'll get your boot off my tire I'll be going."

By the time Jennifer emerged from the bathroom, North Star was history.

"Follow that truck," he'd said.

She drove north, her double horse trailer in tow. The whole country was fenced, she explained. Big ranches with water running through them. They wouldn't find wild horses this far north.

Soon she stopped talking, and when he didn't talk she tried the radio and when there was nothing to pick up, she punched the tape deck. "Ow, ow, ow," she crooned coyotelike.

She turned at Cora, population 12, then took the road back into the mountains. They drove in silence through a hailstorm and later through the sun flashing in and out among the pines.

After the river the road swung along the ridge and turned to mud. Jennifer switched to four-wheel drive and eased it over the small craters. Then the sky turned to slate and the wind came up. They were up high now. The trees thinned and the grass took on an unnatural sheen. Outcroppings of rock jutted everywhere, with stunted trees curling right out of the stone. Snow clung in large fields, piling up over the streams. Everything dripped or ran free like an earthen dam bursting. Before them lay the peaks, monochrome and godlike.

"Stop here," he said.

There was no way a semitrailer could have made it that far. For a second a sense of calm claimed him. "We lost him," he said.

That evening they made camp and he caught two fish. After dinner they sat by the fire.

"What's with the gun?" he asked.

She had just cleaned the cylinder on her classic Colt .44 revolver and was sighting it between his eyes.

She's going to kill me, he thought. That's why she turned back there at Cora.

"A woman can't be too careful," she said.

"Animals?" he asked.

She smiled. "Two-legged."

At dawn he'd got a fire going by loading twigs on a wadded copy of the *Sporting News*. Coffee grounds and water from a jug. Sourdough. He lit a cigarette. He added wood.

From the grub box a skillet and fish knife. From the ice chest the two brookies he'd snagged last evening. The fish lay headless and gutted on the tailgate. Corn oil spat in the pan while he slapped the fish in cornmeal. Potatoes he wrapped in tin foil and buried in the ashes.

As a cook he appreciated something going on while he paid attention to details. Things belonged to places. Skillet, for instance. It was important to rub it with grease and that it be kept in darkness. He wanted to sing to it but decided against waking Jennifer. Instead he just said howdy and turned the fish.

Crows squawking in the trees. Adrian had told him about birds. "East coast birds sing," she'd said. "In Wyoming they retch."

Just as the sun broke over the ridge he heard it, rumbling like buffalo. It came from way down the valley and ricocheted off the rocks like rifle reports. As it got closer the earth filled with it and shook. For a moment he didn't know whether to run or fall down. Then it came, a cloud blowing out of the trees, or dropped upon them. He started for the truck. "Jennifer," he yelled. It was too late.

He slammed the door just as the herd charged out of the trees. There must have been a hundred of them, all crazy and steam-blowing, and no Ford body was going to discourage them. The stallion appeared in the windshield, shook its head and reared. When it came down its forelegs banged the hood.

Boyd fell to the floor and listened to the horses. For a few minutes the earth rumbled while overhead God hovered and spoke in a human tongue.

"You down there," He said.

The herd was gone. Around him all the trees were whipped up and yelling from the chopper blades.

"You're too high," said God. "Find another place to camp." Then the chopper screwed itself back into the sky and roared off.

It was quiet. Boyd was motionless on the floor, staring into the guts of the dashboard when he saw it. Slowly, he reached up behind the steering column and felt the bag taped to the shelf just above the ignition wiring. Jennifer's stash—a pound at least, wrapped and bound. Opening it, he inhaled the black, hard substance. Black tar, they called it in Phoenix, uncut heroin from Mexico. It smelled just like a tin of D. W.'s snouse.

When he got down from the truck, there was no sign of anybody. The fish in the skillet lay smoking on the fire, unmoved. Jennifer's tent remained unruffled. All around the site the earth was pocked but nothing was disturbed.

"Jennifer," he called. He ran to the tent and unzipped it. "Hey," he yelled.

She was gone. Beside her sleeping bag, an overturned sack of clothes, flashlight, maps, and paperback westerns. Wrapped in its gunbelt and kept warm inside the down bag, was her gun.

He went back to the fire and turned the fish. He laid back the meat and drew out the spines, perfect, white, and intact. A breeze came up and wrinkled the aspens. It would be a warm day, he thought. When he looked up it startled him to see a rider appear blurry through the fire. He stood stone-still as the horse calmly took its time through the camp. The rider was made up like a cowboy: boots, chaps, ten-gallon hat, and cheeks bulging with chaw. It was Al Ling, the Chinaman. Slowly he passed out of the fire, behind the pickup, and came out, flowing with the horse, slow and lazy, not pushing the river. At the edge of the clearing he looked back and, barely touching his hat, nodded.

Suddenly the wind went down and the fire died. Everything turned to smoke.

TEN

▼▼▼▼▼ BOYD SAT EATING TROUT and watching the *Sporting News* flex in the ashes. Springtime in these mountains was the time of blizzards, not baseball. There'd been a stampede of wild horses where there wasn't supposed to be. You won't find herds this far north, his client had told him. Then she'd disappeared. That was the story here. Follow the horses.

He pulled up stakes, tossed everything into the truck, and unhitched the trailer. He'd follow the road back to the stream, then keep north. Horses drank water, he thought.

He was entering the case now. He'd drive deeper into it and collect its parts, and finally he'd land right in its middle. Then he'd write it down and the *Stampede* would buy it. Or he'd sell to the highest bidder. Denver maybe, or the *New York Times*. Hell, he'd syndicate the sucker.

He flicked on the radio for news. News, he craved it like his first cigarette. News and the scores.

Instead he got static.

They'll be back, he thought. Another herd of horses and the

same chopper. God would zoom down out of North Star and scare up another herd.

He drove two hours before stopping. The canyon grew craggy and the trees sparser. Snow lay piled beside the road and in places drifted high as the bumper. Near noon he stopped and ate lunch in the truck.

Even from the road he could hear the water. He'd heard how in the old days the railroad dammed the streams so that in spring the sheer force of the runoff exploded the dams, sending the logs crashing downstream. A hundred miles below they were fished out to make ties.

He heard shots, several, at first bunched, then sporadic. Speeding, he swerved to avoid a snow drift and instead hit a log. The front end shuddered and the truck rolled backward.

The shots were closer. From the gunrack he grabbed Jennifer's 30.06 and binoculars and started at a trot. The road swung higher into a narrow gap in the rocks, switched back along the mountain, then suddenly dropped off into a ravine that was hooked together by a hairpin curve and a bridge.

At the bottom was the diesel-semi from Farson, on its side. The trailer had broken free and lay overturned, half in the water. The bridge's log railing looked like match sticks smeared with the red paint of the truck. All over lay the dead horses. They were on the rocks and in the grass and some half in the water, the blood running from huge gashes. The wounded struggled to get up but fell back and kicked. They were crying.

The shots came from an automatic. Marlboro put short bursts into each horse while Ling used a rifle. The two walked in the high grass, stooping to check the wounded then firing, Ling taking aim while Marlboro shot from the hip. Through binoculars Boyd could make out their faces. Marlboro's eyes were glazed, his mouth gnarled in speech. Ling gazed between shots, almost bemused.

Their work took them finally over behind a grassy knoll on the far side of the creek. The grass was so green it was blue under the gray sky. Horse blood made good fertilizer, Boyd thought. He would call this place Dead Horse Canyon. He would fix it on the map.

His gaze lifted into the trees, the aspens spangling in the breeze that carried the scent of rain. He aimed the binoculars in a circle over the east slope until he got it. He adjusted focus and latched on. It was Ling's appaloosa, he recognized it from that morning. The idea struck like a thunderclap. Boyd Sherman, welcome to the horse-rustling business.

He locked the rifle and descended. The downhill going was so fast he had to catch himself on trees. He decided on coming down diagonally so that he'd approach the horse at an angle. He would keep to cover.

He was close now. He approached in a crouch, each step measured. At last he knelt beside the water. It was steaming with horse blood. He was stealing the prize. He would ride the appie back to camp and offer it to his chief. And Follet would give him a bride. Adrian, without the bullshit.

"Attaboy," he whispered to the gelding, giving him plenty to sniff. When he unwound the lead rope, Marlboro and Ling were staring straight at him. They hadn't seen him yet. Suddenly he was a horse. Horses didn't think; rather they thought in a mixture of sky, shadow, light, and spirits rushing. Horses were crazy.

The appie snorted.

The wind came up suddenly and moaned down the canyon, rattling the trees. Instead of firing, they turned away, surveying the slaughter.

Now, thought Boyd.

He looped the reins over the horse's neck and climbed up. "Giddy-up," he said. He made clucking sounds in his throat; he kicked. "Giddy-up."

Again, the horse snorted.

All at once the wind died and the trees went into suspended animation. "Hey, you," Marlboro shouted. He had spotted Boyd, raised his gun and squeezed. Nothing. It was Ling who got off the first round. Boyd heard it slam into a tree.

The horse bolted.

"Goddammed gun," said Marlboro.

A second shot ranged far uphill. "Shoot, shoot," shouted Ling.

"That's what I'm trying," yelled Marlboro.

"Bronco! He steal Bronco."

"We'll get him," raged his partner.

In an instant, Boyd lost the reins. He squeezed the saddle horn so tightly his hands ached. For a second he was a kamikaze pilot—so much intent riveted on wipeout, the dials turned up full and his life rising to meet him like a ghost.

Then came the rock, where the mountain got serious, granite slabs shooting up like wisdom teeth. Hang on, he thought. Give this horse anything he wants.

Bronco lunged. Vertically.

Boyd hated the sky without the lull of gravity. In the next instant he was earthbound. Something beeped in his head and the earth rolled over. Ghosts were trying to kill him. He'd sidled up to them all his life. He'd been a regular escort service for ghosts. He took them out, he took them to bed. They swarmed over his body like dogs lapping at blood in the dust. Jennifer was a ghost; Bronco, a ghost. Together they had thrown him.

He hurt too bad to rest. His left side throbbed and he felt nauseated. Cowboying was for boys, he thought. He listened to the horse breathing and watched the sky. He was in the open now. The chopper would be alerted and a posse would follow. Dammit, he thought. He'd lost the rifle.

Behind the saddle was a canvas roll containing bedding and

poncho. All the leather was plain and functional, no fancy tooling. He checked the cinch and roll tie and climbed up.

He found a game trail that wandered halfway up the slope, then veered with the mountain into thick pine. The damp earth was thick with deer tracks. When he'd come out of the trees he edged around a meadow and began climbing again. From there he could see the semi, just a red speck in the canyon below. He dismounted and scanned the site with binoculars but saw no one. Some of the horses they had not even bothered to finish off.

As his eyes zigzagged up the slope, he saw them, Marlboro and Co., crazy people who didn't give a damn about nobody, guys who threw away their lives and took up schemes. The kind of guys that built towns smack dab in the middle of nowhere, who ran those towns and signed your checks.

He hated success when it came dressed up as virtue. He hated anybody who tried to fix things that were none of their business. He liked people in trouble, people whose lives had blown a hole and they knew it. The rest of them were coming for him, making inroads behind his back. All his life he'd wanted to spook a sonofabitch.

But he was never angry enough. Or big enough. Or he didn't have a gun. And right now Jennifer's .44 was back in the truck.

Focused in his binocs they were looking right at him. Ling held a high-powered canon with a scope. He was drawing a bead.

Boyd ducked just as Ling squeezed the trigger. Instantly, the rock above Boyd's head came apart. I need a hat, he thought. He'd seen some nice ones in town.

But first he needed a gun, and to get one meant getting back to the truck. He loosened the reins and had just crawled back into the saddle when God appeared. The chopper roared straight up out of the ground. Bronco reared into the sky.

Trapped by a monster that flattened grass and growled like a bear, Bronco lunged.

Instantly they were bounding straight down the other side of the mountain like they'd been spun out of a propeller. Rocks and sage burst off the mountain as if it were strip-mined. Below them the pines reared up and for a second it felt like they'd left the mountain, that man and horse had abandoned earth and entered the rainbow.

"Give it up," said God.

More shots. Boyd leaned back and prayed. Bronco, cosmic courier, "we deliver." Horse medicine was flight, wind, and seed pouch, aerial photography.

"Pull up," said God.

Bronco put down his flaps and went into a slide, skidding down the mountain, rocks banging and a cloud of dust, his hind legs tucked underneath and plowing. Boyd didn't breathe until they hit the road.

"Safe," he said, blinking.

The chopper jerked straight up as if snagged by a skyhook. It circled once more, then shot out of there. Boyd rode into the protection of trees and listened. No sign of Marlboro and Co. Besides Bronco's panting, not a sound but the trees and the faint gurgling of water. He waited, watching the horse's ears scan like a gun site. The rain he'd glimpsed from the top was overhead now. He listened to the first patter in the trees, a few drops coming through the canopy. The aroma of sage coiled like steam off the canyon floor. On the opposite ridge, gold light and a rainbow.

ELEVEN

▼▼▼▼▼ "WHOA," HE SAID.

He got down off the horse and continued on foot. Smoke hung in the trees like gauze. Campfire, he thought.

His client's truck, unmoved, unchanged.

Tied to a tree were two horses.

And a pup tent. He watched the wind play tricks with it, then subside. No movement.

He figured on situating himself between the tent and the creek. If they appeared before Boyd could get to the truck, he'd hang back and wait. And if they spotted him first? If they were unarmed, charge them.

He waited till dark to go to work. He circled back of the horses and lay low behind the pickup. He listened to his breath, its shallowness and the catch it registered when the truck door unlatched and swung open. There, he thought, slipping inside and extinguishing the cab light.

The gun laid coiled in leather like a snake under the seat. He felt the braille of keys until one matched the steering column and he began slowly pumping the gas. He pumped fifty times, clutch engaged, the shift in neutral. Switch on.

Suddenly the door swung open, the cab light blinking and the radio spitting static at ninety decibels. Outside, a dog went crazy. Boyd jammed into reverse and dug in. That's when the door slammed against a tree. By now a flashlight was darting all over the windshield. Boyd waved his gun, prepared to shoot anything that moved. He flicked on the headlights, shifted, and shot forward. Right there, dead in his brights—"Adrian?" he shouted. "What are *you* doing here?"

She aimed the flashlight up under her chin, grinning ghoulishly like a squaw spirit who devoured men foolish enough to violate her burial mound.

"Hey, don't do that," he said.

She walked back to the fire and added wood. Her body threw a large shadow on the trees. Alone out here she had stopped being a woman. Out here she was a bear, able and cunning, accepting of strangers but vicious when backed against the rocks.

"I got a horse," he said.

"Then you better get him," she said.

"I'll get him," he said.

He came back with Bronco in tow and unsaddled him. "Hold this," said Adrian, handing him the flashlight. She ran her hands over the horse. "You've got to dry him off."

"There wasn't time," he said.

She was checking his forelegs. "Boyd, you've got to walk him before he catches pneumonia."

She walked the horse around the fire, brushed him, then slapped on a blanket. After tying him with the others, she came back with his bridle. "He's got a hard mouth," she said.

"Sorry, I'll take him back."

"You didn't let him drink after that run, did you?"

"I'm not stupid," he said.

"Good," she said. "He can use some water then."

She poured water from a jug into a pot and took it to the horse. When she set it down the others wanted a piece of the action. Boyd watched her talk to them. To train was to control appetite. She was good at it. She demanded results and she got them. It was impossible being a husband to a creature like that, he thought.

Right then he realized his attraction to the case. Inside the fact of stolen horses and a dead husband lay enormous space. The case was so open you could drive a horse trailer through it. He'd slept with his client. In one night he'd stored enough hand-held erotic images to last him into senility. Strictly low-budget.

The case afforded a girl and a sense of movement. These were the dreams of pharoahs, of T'ang Dynasty rulers. He had dressed history up so that it promised marvelous spells and rendezvous. His birth sign was water.

Adrian came back from the horses and gave water to her sheep dog. "We need water," she said.

He could sense her standing behind him. She tossed an empty canteen at his feet. For a moment he lay smoking, listening to the dog's lapping, and farther back, the horses.

Taking the flashlight, he slung the canteen over his shoulder and headed for the creek. The trail dipped through the trees and ran out in the tall grass that bordered the water. The dew soaked his pants and made his boots squeak. At the bank he dipped the canteen into the current, ice-cold, green under the light. Beneath him lay gold-spotted stones, a fish. A brookie, all right, twelve, fourteen inches maybe, aiming north just to stay even with the current. All around him suddenly he felt the gaze of animals. He switched off the light. Blackout, then gradually, his eyes adjusting as if emerging from their sockets—stars.

Back at the fire he set another log and made coffee. "Are you alone?" he asked.

"I got Bud," she said.

The dog perked up at the sound of his name, then resumed snoozing.

"Anybody else?"

"What do you think?"

He had to stop and think. He hardly ever spoke to her when it meant something. Instead he tried out lines meant to provoke her. It was a habit.

"I don't know," he said.

She was leaning by the fire brushing her teeth. Sacajawea with Crest, twenty percent fewer cavities. She took water from the canteen, washed hands and face and rinsed. "There never was anyone else," she said. Then she rousted Bud and together they entered the tent. There followed a small commotion until they were settled.

The wind came up and the fire sputtered. He considered adding another log but what was the point? Instead he dug out the divorce papers from his pack. Four months and still not signed. She didn't even ask him anymore. He smoothed out the creases and laid the papers on the fire. Dragon, he thought, listening to the moaning in the pines. Sky dragon, man and woman dragon.

"Whoa," he said. He had come to the place.

He remembered when he was a kid, his father had gone to Chicago on business and come back with a surprise. It was a book, the *Golden Book of Billy and Sue at the Ranch* or *Billy and Sue's Vacation,* he couldn't remember.

There was this kid Billy and his sister who lived back East in a city. School's out and Mom and Dad have a big surprise. "Billy, Sue, how'd you like to visit your Uncle Luke's ranch at Gopher Wells, just the two of you?"

"Oh, boy, would we?"

Next there's a train ride and suddenly, Gopher Wells. Uncle Luke and Aunt Sarah wave from the pickup. It's a red truck that's twisted like it's half-melted, with bald tires and headlights big as moons. The old folks say, "Reckon you're hungry." They let the kids ride in back. Everywhere there's cowboys and windmills and sage, and all the dirt looks gold.

At the ranch Aunt Sarah outfits them in genuine wrangler duds with pointy boots, spurs, and chaps, and fringe and silver buckles and ten-gallon hats. "Well, look at you," says Luke.

Out behind the barn, two ponies—pintos—and saddles with silver studs.

"Mine's Danny," says Billy. "Danny Boy."

"And mine's Rainbow," says Susie.

"Put your feet in the stirrups," says Luke. "Say giddy-up."

In just a few minutes Billy's jump-mounting while Susie's working on barrel-jumping and trick-riding. She's got this one where she rides backward full out while shooting a line of tin cans with a Winchester.

"Don't that beat all," says Uncle Luke.

Aunt Sarah whips the dinner gong and all the boys come running. She serves up chili, refritos, and pie. Uncle Luke takes off his hat. "Heavenly Father, thanks for my new teeth, amen."

Cowboys wear mustaches and answer to names like Chester and Milo. There's Frank the foreman, and Jesse and Dick, all good men with a six-gun and a bullwhip. They sing songs while Rusty plays harmonica.

Billy and Susie fall asleep in the barn listening to bats in the eaves. Tomorrow they'll punch cows and maybe race to the river.

"Rise 'n shine," says Luke. When he talks it's like smoke signals. He'll probably die of bowel cancer.

After breakfast, Billy and Susie saddle up and ride out under the Lazy Bar brand that tops the front gate. "Last one to the river's a varmit," yells Billy. He's heard the hands talk like that. He likes their words that ooze like slugs of tobacco, words like double back, partner, grub, and gun play. He slaps Danny Boy on the rump and hunkers mean in the saddle.

"Look at me, Susie!"

The kid wins going away. There's only one problem. Danny Boy doesn't seem to want to whoa. He plows through the river and leaps out the other side. Hang on, Billy.

Suddenly, the horse rears. Danny Boy spots a rattler and jumps right out of his saddle, dumping Billy in a culvert. The rattler strikes. "Oww," says Billy.

Just then an Indian brave with a single feather comes out from behind a rock. He picks up the snake by the tail, twirls it like a lasso, and lets it fly.

"I didn't know those varmits could strike up to twice their length," says Billy.

The Indian inspects the puncture marks on the boy's arm and grunts approval. He takes his headband and makes a tourniquet. Then with his knife he cuts a small cross and commences to suck.

By now Susie's pulled up all out of breath. "Leave my brother alone," she threatens.

The Indian spits out a mouthful of milky venom and stares at the girl. "Ugh," he says. He goes toward her and yanks her blond hair. When it doesn't come off, he's horrified.

"It's okay, Susie," says her brother.

Next the brave checks her teeth, then moves his hands over her. When he's satisfied, he turns to Billy and, man-to-man, offers him his single feather. "Eagle," he says, "you," pointing to make clear the connection. "Me—squaw."

The feather for the boy's sister, that's the equation. "Susie," he says, "my friend wants to take you with him."

"I don't want to go," she shouts.

Billy's mad. "Didn't you always want to be an Indian princess? Huh?"

She begins to cry. Billy's got to think fast. What would Uncle Luke do, he considers. "Protect your own," the old man had said.

Billy shakes his head. "No deal," he says.

The Indian shouts things the boy doesn't understand. Billy takes his sister's hand. "C'mon, Susie, I'll race you back to the ranch."

Just as they mount their horses, the Indian shrieks and snaps into a coiled rattler. The horses rear and take off, bounding so fast the wind gags the kids. The ride back is so smooth it reminds Billy of rolling in bed. Somewhere in another room Mom and Dad are snoring. . . .

The campfire coals flared for a second, then dimmed. "Adrian?" he called. "Are you awake?" When there was no answer he wondered if he'd really said it or just thought it. He thought so loudly he was sure people heard him.

In the middle of the night the wind came up and he got the fire going. Too cold to lie still, he began smoking and dancing, his hands crammed into his pockets, chanting *huh-ya-ya-ya, huh-ya-ya-ya*. Finally he ripped into Adrian's pack and found jerky. In a leather sling, the Marlin 30–30 lever action her father had given her for her birthday. August something, just before Boyd had left the apartment for good. She sat in the kitchen by herself. "Virgo," she'd sneered. "You know what that means? It means horny."

He sniffed the barrel. She'd been shooting, all right. Adrian at it again. Woman saves estranged husband, then leaves him to freeze, goes the headline. He liked a manly woman.

"No, you don't," she'd said.

"Whaddya mean?"

"You want a maid, someone who'll screw on demand and not

squawk. Someone to adore you. And when you don't get it you take your toys and run. Boyd, I'm not your problem."

Adrian, his problem. Who'd fought with him and showed no respect. "I don't want your balls," she'd yelled. It was at a restaurant in Salt Lake. "You keep them," she'd said. "They wouldn't look good on me."

He was hunkered by the fire devouring jerky when he stopped chewing. "What are you doing?" he asked.

Adrian stood wrapped in an Indian blanket. She didn't move. The wind came up and the fire turned on its side.

"Miss Jennifer's been talking," she said. "She got drunk at the Trails and blabbed how she and you were fixing to search for horses. Told everybody she's offering a reward. I told you she's a bitch."

Boyd tossed another log. She was right, he thought. She'd warned him.

"The man in Cora said you'd be up here," she continued. "I tracked you from there. Pickup and a horse trailer, it was easy."

Adrian had never spoken much. It was just that he'd never noticed it till Wyoming. In Wyoming there wasn't noise to fill the gaps. A white living room and a color TV. Cable news and weather. Last summer he'd thought of writing a book about sports but couldn't get started. There was nothing to say.

She did tell him about D. W. Ling. Ling was the latest in a long tradition of Chinese godfathers. She told how a hundred years ago the Chinese came to lay rails, how they settled in town to mine coal, how their number grew into a ghetto comprised of tar-paper shacks and opium parlors. How in reaction to management's unfair wage scale, white miners charged through the community, killing and destroying in what was called the Chinese Rebellion. Adrian told him. Adrian who wouldn't go to the Trails. "Bad news," she'd said.

She checked the horses, then made bacon and eggs. "Got yourself a trail horse," she said.

"Name's Bronco. Got him from Al Ling."

"I know," she said.

They ate in silence, letting the fire die down.

"Where you headed now?" she asked.

"North Star."

"North Star's all over," she said.

"Whaddya mean?"

"It's a corporation. They've got pasture, oil fields, uranium, everything."

"Who's they?"

"State guys, federal maybe, who knows? Corporate types, white shirts and tax shelters. Guys who've never been on a horse in their lives. They think about votes, lobbying, and stuff like that. You catch my drift?"

"Man-See-Horse," said Boyd.

"What?"

"Chinese," he said. "It's on the menu at the Trails. Doloras told me."

"Oh," she said, "you're learning Chinese now. Medicine Dog needs a good laundry, you know."

Boyd tossed the dregs of the coffee. "Come with me," he said.

"What for? The reward?"

"For the horses."

TWELVE

▼▼▼▼▼ AT DAWN THEY SADDLED their horses, loaded the pack horse, and rode north. Soon the road ended and it began to rain, and as they climbed higher it turned to snow. They took the trail and Bud followed.

Farther on, the trail began switching back and forth like the dragon's tail so that at each bend he could make out where they'd just been. Below lay Dead Horse Canyon and the road winding south beneath the mist into the broad valley. Above, the clouds stampeded eastward, the thin gauze peeled back from the sky and the dark herds falling through and splayed just above his head. Their spirits rode in back with him. When he cupped his hands to warm them, he smelled fish, mineral, and moss from the stream.

"In the northern darkness there is a fish and his name is K'un." Chuang Tzu, *Free and Easy Wandering*. How long had it been? The Tao could not be written or uttered. If you're reading this, it said, then this ain't it. He liked that idea. It was what attracted him to the old masters. It meant not having to do something about his drinking.

Later the booze took over and there wasn't time for Chuang and the basic writings. Then he'd sobered up. After that even the buddhas smelled of bourbon.

Trouble ahead, said the *Ching*. Abide in what endures. No blame. The words attracted ghosts, that was their aggregate meaning. Chinese characters were the most haunted. He thought of all those coolies working the mines, their sleep twitching with the vowels of their dragons. Underground you could hear the chaos, the ghosts rumbling in the walls.

Excellent horses. Follow the woman to the horses. Horse and dragon: Creative, the Arousing.

Neither of them spoke in the falling snow. It whited out everything but the rocks and the close-up insides of things—coat liners and pockets, the overhang of his parka hood.

He guzzled from the canteen. Cigarettes and snow dried him out. "Cigarettes keep you two thousand feet higher," Adrian had told him. At this altitude he wasn't even touching the earth.

"Everyday work like Chinaman," Dragon Lady had said. This constant climbing, every step dogged by ghosts. Climb or die. Shake out the ghosts, their sweetness that climbs into your sleeping bag, into your clothes, under your fingernails.

Adrian rode on ahead believing in God. God the broad back, the crunch of the ax, leather cinch, and buckle. You fastened to God like mounting a wild horse. You held on. That was her goodness, her strength. It's what he envied.

He rode behind, watching the pack horse, the sway of supplies in rhythm to plodding, Adrian somewhere up there, attached by rope, stepping right through herself into nothing.

Follow the horses. Follow the woman to the horses.

They climbed for hours until the snow piled so high they had to break trail. Here they alternated horses to preserve strength. At last, whiteout, and a slight tugging of line. "Hold my horse," she said.

He stood holding the reins, freezing, withdrawing deeper into his hood and finally closing his eyes. Deep inside he saw her. This was what it was like to die out here, he thought.

It was when he opened his eyes that he realized something had happened. Bud had disappeared. What he'd seen was not Adrian. Adrian had taken her horse. This was a squaw with a baby on her back. "I've come back," she said. Or she hadn't talked but made a gesture, some motion of assurance. In the bulk of his bear body he felt her touch him.

"Boyd," said Adrian, "listen to me. There's a cave on the other side of those rocks. We can stay there."

He felt her fasten the line to his belt and pull into the wind. Again he was moving but could not feel his legs. Nor could he remember the day of the week or where he was going. But he knew those things were out there.

The cave was a cleft in the rock that permitted entrance to one person at a time. It was too squat for horses. "Horse entrance is up above," she said, leading the way. Together they struggled getting the horses over the rock, unpacking, tugging, cajoling, until by pulling the reins they squeezed inside.

First was an earthen stairway and the white eye of the escape hatch below. They stood holding each other and panting with the horses. The wind whistled as through a chipped tooth. "It's okay," she gasped. "I know this place."

He followed her until it was almost completely dark. From there he could hear the stream roaring at the foot of the mountain, and closer, the scamper of animals. He felt Bud's wet nose on the back of his hand.

She banged her flashlight till it came on, then handed it to him. Next she produced a kerosene lamp from her pack. She lit it and adjusted the wick. That's when he saw the writings, messages, hundreds of them scrawled on the rock. *Four day storm*, said one. *Waiting for others*. Signed, *Jewett '82*. *Broken leg. Bear ate my horse. Elza gone ahead.*

Adrian said it was old. "Kid Curry," she said, pointing to it. "Real name Harvey Logan."

She spoke of the Outlaw Trail: Canada through Montana with Wyoming stops at Hole-in-the-Wall, Robber's Roost, and Atlantic City. Then into Utah at Brown's Hole and Glen Canyon, much of it the Old Spanish Trail, the Escalante, old Indian trails running parallel and bisecting the Union Pacific, all the way to El Paso. One stop was Silver City, home of William Bonney.

Having cleared the place of shell casings, they built a fire from twigs. "I used to come here with Vern," she said. "He knew a man who rode with Kid Curry. He says it's haunted. Outlaws are superstitious."

The cave had been first used by Civil War deserters. Before that, the Indians. The Powder River gang had used it for ten years. In the late '70s Frank and Jesse James hid out here after pulling a train job near Carbon.

"See that there?" she said, pointing. "That's Isom Dart. He was a black man who broke horses for the Wild Bunch. He could read and write. Outlaws were smart. Elza Lay was college-educated. He planned their jobs."

Then came Charlie Siringo, the Pinkerton who infiltrated the gang and busted some of them. He'd written novels. "Tom Horn got Isom," she said. "Tom Horn was crazy."

She told about Cleophas Dowd, a Catholic priest, rancher, detective, U.S. marshall, and horse rustler who spoke seven languages and a bunch of Indian dialects. It was Cleophas who named Harry Longbaugh the Sundance Kid.

Boyd lay back and gazed at the names sputtering above the flames. He was warm now. He hoped the storm would rage for a long time.

"That's a lot of horse rustling," he said.

"There's been horse rustlers since before horses," said Adrian. "Medicine dogs."

"That's Indian for horse."

"Maybe. Or maybe horse is just what we call our brand of medicine dog."

Boyd got up and pulled a charred stick from the fire. He would write his own message to the future.

REWARD
of $5000 for information leading to the capture & arrest of Boyd Sherman. Accompanied by wife Adrian. Both armed & dangerous.

Adrian read the message. "Wanted for what?"

"The murder of Rusty Landrus."

"You've been set up," said Adrian.

He lay down on the sleeping bag and smoked. He watched the shadows jump over the words he'd written. "I saw something back there," he said.

Adrian rolled over and faced him. "An Indian woman with a baby."

"What are you talking about?"

"I've seen her. She's buried east of here on the reservation. Vern thinks I'm crazy."

"Who's buried?"

"Sacajawea. That's who you saw. Sacajawea and Baptiste."

Boyd looked at her. She glowed. He didn't know if he should laugh or decide once and for all that splitting up with her was the best thing that could have happened. He looked back into the fire. "You mean I really saw her?" he said.

"What do you think?"

"You never told me."

"You'd never believe me," she said. "To you I was just a college dropout. You never had to get serious. You're a pro. What you didn't count on was that I'd come to mean something to you. That's when you ran. And that's too bad, Boyd, because we mean something to each other."

When he didn't answer, she reached out and touched his face. "You like being a ghost, don't you?"

"Maybe."

"You like the dead. Private detective is the perfect job for you."

She sat up and fed the fire. "So here you are," she said, "stuck in the snow with Sacajawea. You'll need her to get out of here."

She had him there. He had no idea where they were. North. North Star. Wyoming, the outer kingdom. Out of the world.

"Get some sleep," she said. "I'll keep watch."

The last thing he remembered was that he didn't like her keeping watch. He trusted her, all right; it was himself he wasn't sure about. The walls separating ghost from flesh and dream from duty weren't exactly reliable. He felt her invade his sleep and adjust the furniture, tossing out all the ashtrays and magazines. She'd see him missing these things, he feared, as if sleep were a spell put on him, the sleep of outlaws.

In the dream there were horses roaming in giant seasonal whorls like the stars. Next he was in a shelter with a woman. She'd stretched her hands over his back, urging him, grasping for all his life in a jolt.

Sacajawea, he called her.

He was soaking wet and his penis was lead pipe. He touched himself to bring her back, to fix her to the earth beneath him. He would not ask Adrian to help him. He'd shoot into his fist and stop breathing.

"Boyd," she called, turning toward him.

He would tell her it was a dream but she wouldn't let him. She rolled into his bag and tugged at his belt. "Here," she said.

"What are you doing?"

When she smiled it was the first time he'd seen her without shame since Phoenix. She pulled off layers of wool, her breasts shivering with cold. "Gonna use that thing before it goes away," she said.

Naked, she straddled him and slipped him inside her. He was entering history, where the names and faces changed and the tails of buffalo began to swish.

She pulled the open bag around her shoulders but again it fell back. Boyd watched her above him, the flames rolling over her, abandoning herself.

That's when it happened. It came in slow motion but he couldn't stop it. She had penetrated the dream with arms and legs outstretched. She'd made it joint property and met him there on equal terms. "Adrian," he called, pulling her down. Rolling over on her he thrust once and came. They lay in the dirt.

He did not know until his own spasms had subsided that she was crying. "I love you," he said. "I've never stopped."

She didn't open her eyes. Tears streamed into her hair and finally she smiled. Only after a long time of seeing her like that did he realize it was Sacajawea.

THIRTEEN

▼▼▼▼ "DAMMIT," SHE SAID. "I just got my period." She pulled on her clothes and headed outside.

Bear and sex went together, he thought. Just a trace of female traveled like a rifle shot. Bears went for it, climbed right out of their skins and exposed themselves as bear people, the secret clan, bothered by the vague memory of having been in there, in the uterine world, its warmth and steam of eggs sloughed off. Grizzlies killed for it.

Bud began whining. "What's wrong with you?" Boyd asked. Voices.

Four men came out of the darkness dragging a deer. They had Adrian. Boyd went to her but a big guy in the lead stopped him with a kick to the chest. When he opened his eyes, one of them was struggling to take her rifle from her. "Bastards," she shouted. Boyd dove for the young one who wore a crunched-up western hat with a feather. The kid wheeled around and gulped; he'd taken Boyd's fist in the groin. The next thing Boyd felt was a large set of knuckles. Again he got up and felt his teeth crack. He staggered with his face in his hands and keeled over.

When he came to, Adrian spooned up beans and poured coffee. Then she went to a rock and sat with her knees drawn up. At dinner Boyd chewed once, then spat it out. He'd forgotten about his teeth. "Damn," he said, dropping his plate.

"Hey, dog meat," said the big guy, "you don't like your woman's cooking?"

"You insulting her?" challenged one of the others.

They watched him without curiosity. Having already measured him, there was nothing to understand. Now they could relax. They lay on the ground pouring whiskey into tin cups.

"Where you headed?" asked the big guy. He lay against a log, his hair in braids and his belly inflated. He wore a bronze belt buckle that said "Wyoming Native."

"North Star," Boyd replied.

The big guy offered the bottle. "North Star? You got business there?"

"Looking for a job."

"A job? What kinda job?"

Boyd reached into his pocket for a cigarette. "Gimme one of them," said the kid. Then the others chimed in and Boyd handed over the pack.

The big guy swallowed from the bottle and again extended it toward Boyd. Again, no thanks.

"What kinda work you do?"

Boyd looked at Adrian. She'd been messed with, all right. They'd taken turns. He looked the Indian right in the eye and said, "Cowboy."

A smile seemed to pass through the big man's eyes like headlights. He nodded. "We're Arapaho," he said. "You're on our land."

The talk quickly turned to deer. Arapaho were free to shoot deer out of season on the reservation; that was tribal law. Today's kill was a large buck. He'd watched them slit its throat. The hunter's name was Emory, the young one, the one with the feather. It was his first deer and the first shot had been to the belly. He'd chased it a long ways before dropping it with a round to the head. The men teased him about it. It was only after they'd gone back for the horses that they'd come across Adrian.

Emory lay the animal out sprawling with its legs in the air, severed its genitals, and tossed them to Bud. He next inserted the tip of his buck knife into the wound and sliced upward toward the breast bone. When he pulled back the skin, the organs sloshed toward the hindquarters.

Emory was bloodied to the elbows. He took a snort off the bottle and grinned. He had no front teeth and a face shot with acne. He grabbed hold of the antlers and again dropped the carcass over a log. Then he plunged his knife with both hands and sawed first laterally, then straight up through the ribs. At one point the bone was so tough he pulled free and stabbed again with a war cry. The others laughed and whistled.

The boy measured what was left of the whiskey and drained it. What happened next seemed natural, like drunken slow-motion replays of a heavyweight taking a terrible blow to the head. Instead of cutting away, the boy dragged the blade toward himself for more leverage. When the bone snapped the blade entered him just inside the thigh. The men sat stunned.

Adrian got to him first. She whipped out her bandana and cinched the boy's thigh. "Get me rags," she ordered. The men groped around the fire, cursing.

The kid refused to lie still. Pale-faced, ugly, and whimpering, he beat the ground with his fists. When she pushed him back he became hysterical, screeching in Arapaho. Finally he threw up.

Boyd sat on him and held the flashlight while she rinsed the wound. For a second there was the muscle before the blood spurted again. Blood splashed over the ground and formed pools. She tried sopping it with the rags but it was no use. "Help me," she said. Boyd tightened the boy's tourniquet as she instructed.

Adrian headed for the horses. "Get out of my way," she barked, pushing the horses back. She returned with flannel shirts for wrapping. "You're in my light," she said.

Next she ordered them to build up the fire—which they did, signifying a renewal of strength. Two of them dragged in large, snarly branches of windfall while the big guy gutted the deer. Humming to himself he went to work cutting. First he snipped the lungs and set them out. Then he raised the carcass nearly over his head and, with a thunderous cry, slammed it on a rock, breaking the pelvic bone. He cut slits in the hind legs and chopped off a branch to make a gambrel. When he inserted the shaft into the hind slits, one of the others brought line that was then tied to the branch. All three hoisted the deer onto one of the horses. Then, with their backs to the fire, they urinated.

The whole camp smelled of meat and whiskey, as if that alone fueled the fire. "He gonna make it?" asked Boyd.

"I don't know," she sighed.

She splashed her face with water, matting her hair. When she pushed it back there were scratches on her neck.

"Fix him," he said, "then I'll kill him."

She sunk her head between her knees. When she raised it, it was to check on her patient. He was mumbling about going into business with his uncle.

Wyoming Native withdrew the log from the fire and kicked dirt. He moved like a man who'd taken a deep breath and concluded something vast in his mind. He was breaking camp. He stood over Emory. "You ready to ride?" he asked.

"He needs a doctor," said Adrian.

"I'm talking to him," he said.

The big guy signaled the others to get the kid on his feet. He was smiling like an old man who knew better than to argue with a white woman. "So long," he said. He led the horse with the deer and his own horse from the cave. Outside it was clear. Snow covered everything and glowed in the moon. He climbed into his saddle, then waited for the others to help the kid up. Last he fixed the boy's arms around his belly, then spoke to the horse. Within seconds they were gone.

Boyd and Adrian lay down on the bags. The stream seemed louder now, so loud it did not seem they would ever speak again.

"It stopped snowing," he said.

Daylight shot the entrance and landed in a beam high up on the wall. He lay wondering where the Indians were and what it looked like to them. He sensed something both hazardous and peaceful about how they saw things. He would kill them with his bare hands. Adrian would lead him to them. Bird Woman arranged things.

Bird Woman, interpreter, guide, troubleshooter. He had never intended to learn from her. And now they lay in the dark, wrapped in the sound of water, licking their wounds.

"Boyd?" she said.

He raised up on his side and looked at her. In the dark he could see nothing.

"It's not what you think," she said. "They tried to put the kid on me but my period put them off."

For a second he was a mountain man loaded with pelts. As Bird Woman's husband he possessed wealth. Mountain man and squaw was solid economics—no frills.

"Hold me," she whispered.

They lay under the same down, their arms locked and their bladders full. Finally he got up. "It's late," he said. "I don't want us here if they decide to come back."

She sat up as if awakened to another dream with its own terror and narrow escape. "That kid's dead," she said.

She was serious. "Then let's go," he said.

By the time the sun peaked they were northbound, leading their horses, following tracks in the perfect whiteness. The air was so pure it made his eyes smart. He would stare straight down the stovepipes of her tracks and follow. He would trudge along the rail of his breath, moving steady, north by northeast.

Crows flapped in the trees and powder sprinkled down, pocking the surface. No wind anywhere; that meant the tracks would stay for a long time.

In the afternoon the wind came up and visibility shrank. They descended a thousand feet and came upon old ruts that led to a shack. It was an abandoned line shack, its log planking cracked and the chinking gone. The wind moaned so loud it spooked the horses.

Adrian broke out antelope jerky, cheese, and water so cold it gave him a headache. She warmed instant soup on a gas stove and checked the map.

"We're lost," he said.

"I'm not sure," she answered.

He listened to the wind. Last night he had coupled with another body, he thought. And now he was lost in his. Other people were abstract, like ghosts. Adrian was not a ghost because he'd been inside her. That's what all those months without her had done, he decided. It had made him haunted.

He walked around checking the floor ruts for bullets. He'd never been lucky at finding things. He wasn't good at finding constellations in the night sky either. He was good at discovering restaurants.

Like the Happy Trails. For a second he glimpsed himself outside the case, far from men and women in a small town, collected on cold mornings in a place with Chinese subtitles, drinking coffee, reading the papers, and cursing the Bureau of Land Management, Union Pacific, the Russians.

He rocked on his haunches, punching his gloved hand. Finally he snatched up the pan and put it to his lips. "Dammit," he gasped, spilling it.

"What do you expect picking up a hot pan?"

"It's not hot," he said.

"Give it to me."

She set it back on the flame, then looked at him. "Are you okay?" she asked.

He didn't take his eyes off the soup. Chicken broth. Bubbles appeared at the edges. "I don't know," he said. It sounded like the most tragic fact a man could utter. The admission had been swelling inside him like a cancer. "I don't know."

He commenced to breathe in short powerful blows. Everything blurred.

"It's amazing," she said, "how long it takes to boil water at this altitude."

"Yeah," he said. He was chewing his glove.

"Have you noticed how snow melts at twenty above?"

"No," he said.

Then he thought about it. In Wyoming it seemed that snow melted at anything above zero. Suddenly he felt a rule of compensation at work in these mountains. For every hardship there was a tiny fact buried beneath the snow. If you found it, it saved your life.

"I want some soup," he blurted. He said it like it was medicine, something linked to his ancestors. He yanked off his glove and stuck his finger in the pan. "It's hot," he said.

She poured it into cups and they sat against the wall, sipping. Soup was remedy in northern families. Chicken broth and tea. And at bedtime, black tea with a shot of whiskey.

"It's good," he said.

Then he saw it: North Star, circle and compass, carved into the overhead beam. And next to it, the name White Bear. "You see that?" he asked.

"It's North Star's brand."

"This isn't the reservation," he said.

He gulped his soup and smacked his lips. "Let's go," he said.

"What's your hurry?"

"The horses those Indians were riding, they're North Star."

"And they're stolen," she said.

"How do you know?"

"They bragged about it, how they'd ripped off the white man just like in the old days."

The horses stood with their tails to the wind. Mounted, the beasts shook their heads and turned into the teeth of it. Plodding further, they lost the tracks, the trail becoming treacherous. The horses had to pick their spots, and Bud followed in their wake.

They crossed another stream that Adrian guessed connected with the earlier one. Here all the waters connected. Streams and rivers ran uphill and looped and tied themselves in knots. South Fork Creek became the Lower South Fork that later narrowed to the Little South Fork. Water flowed out of these mountains like rays from a star, bursting forth, linking up, changing name and rerouting. They disappeared underground and required rites to bring them out of hiding.

It was the horse talking. At this altitude Boyd's thoughts took in the horse and broke up; they became the horse talking back. Bronco talked on and on, then stopped to remind his rider it was all the same to him, that men were crazy but sometimes they fed you and brushed your back.

"You're no crazier than the Chinaman," said Bronco.

"Tell me about him."

"Forget it. You're all alike."

"Where is Ling?"

"He's underground, listening, saving all this, storing it in vaults. He's not talking."

"Take me to the horses."

End of conversation.

Slow trudging through powder. Up close the snow swirled and grated like sand, the air clear as a fine-tuned engine.

Adrian pulled up and turned in her saddle. "Hear that?" She had out her Marlin. She pointed to a small canyon filled with cottonwoods. "Stay close," she said. It seemed forever before they made it into the trees.

Another stream, smaller than before, and rye grass. Snow stuck to the sides of trees so that they looked sand-blasted. It began to snow, a funnel of it right out of the sunlight.

They tied their horses and stood in the thicket, listening. Suddenly he felt a hand on his shoulder and swung around. She was smiling, her eyes all lit up like she'd had a vision. She pointed beyond the stream into a tangle of trees. Then she drew a map in the snow. They would split up, he heading for the clearing, then coming back on the far side of the stream.

Maneuvers. He had a knife and the enemy was real, a fat Indian who had beat him with his fists and laid hands on his woman. Who'd sat down and talked hunting with him, who wished him well. The enemy was an insane sonofabitch waiting out there. He had to believe that; not to believe it meant suicide. Dead people used to think everybody thought like they did.

He came to a fence and followed it back into the trees. When he came out the other side he saw them, hundreds of them painted against the white hills, heads down and tails swishing, each smoking in the cold like suburban chimneys.

"I'll bet they're all stolen," said Adrian, joining him. They climbed through the fence and moved among them. Adrian recognized some of the brands. They were from all over, she said, some as far as Utah.

In the middle of the herd they found Al Ling, the Chinaman. He was curled up on the ground, his hands frozen into permanent claws and his face collapsed like a prune, a gaping hole in his chest. Large-caliber, up close and personal, say your prayers, Charlie. Ling was underground, all right. And he wasn't talking.

"Man-See-Horse himself," said Boyd.

At the gate were snow-machine tracks trailing into the trees and over the hill. On the sky the wind wrote a letter dictated by the deceased. It asked the white man for mercy and drew the clouds down from Montana like a blanket. Sleep, it said, is what men craved.

FOURTEEN

▼▼▼▼ WHINNY FROM THE TREES.

"Visitors," said Boyd, drawing his revolver. He circled back to their horses while she stayed with the herd. At the stream he heard voices. Big Guy & Co.

The Indians were hoisting the kid into a tree. They had constructed a rope harness and used a horse. When they'd finished fastening him to the branches they paused to urinate. That's when they spotted Adrian. "Hey," they said, "where's your man?"

"Turn around and I'll blow your face off," said Boyd.

He went up behind Big Guy and grabbed his hair. The Indian grunted. "Hey, Cowboy," he said. Meanwhile, Adrian went to the kid's horse and unsheathed her rifle.

Suddenly Big Guy dropped his shoulder and reached for the gun. He barked something in Arapaho. His horse jerked free; Adrian lunged for the reins but fell down. Boyd quickly recovered and again had the Indian by the hair. He pulled him to the ground and pressed the barrel of the revolver between his eyes. "You're White Bear."

"Huh?"

Boyd cocked the hammer. "White Bear."

"Oh, sure."

"Where'd you get the horses?"

"Get what?"

Boyd yanked hard and the brave's eyes widened. The Indian snorted and spat in the white man's eye. Boyd tried spitting back but his mouth suddenly was parched. He brought the gun down on the man's cheek, tearing the skin beneath the eye.

"We got 'em from some white guy," said the other brave.

"Who?"

"A guy called Frampton, I think, yeah."

"What for?"

"Whaddya mean what for?" raged White Bear. "He gave them to us. He said watch for strangers. Hey, I can't see."

Boyd tightened his hold on the hair. "And Ling?"

"He's dead. Frampton shot him."

"For the money? I said for the money?"

"Yeah, the money. Ling delivered the money, then took the herd up."

"Then what happens?"

"They launder the herd. Some goes to Montana for auction. The good ones get sold. Show horses. They take orders from all over. Some they raffle for charity."

Boyd let go of White Bear and watched the kid in the tree rock back and forth. "How long's he been dead?"

"This morning," answered White Bear.

Boyd faced the big guy. "Take me to North Star."

White Bear shrugged.

"You ride for them, you can ride one more time. We're taking this herd in."

The Indian shook his head. "Can't do it," he said.

With a kick to the chest Boyd sent the brave sprawling.

"Boyd—"

Adrian saw something on the hill beyond the pasture. "Snow machine."

"It's Frampton," said White Bear.

"You talk to him," said Boyd. "You tell him North Star wants these horses. You say D. W. Ling's sent people. I'll be in those trees and you'll be in my sights. Got it?"

"Don't do it, Kyle," yelled the other brave.

Again Boyd put the revolver to the man's head. "I'll do it," said White Bear.

The big guy took a handful of snow and pawed it to his eye, which was beginning to close. He examined the blood on his hand while Adrian hustled the others into the trees. Then he stood up. "I'll trade you that deer for one of those cigarettes."

Instead Boyd traded Adrian his revolver for the rifle. "Let's go," he said.

By the sound of it the snow machine would appear just over the rise. White Bear walked the perimeter while Boyd sighted in. He thought to check the chamber and found it empty. Panicky, he found White Bear in his scope as if looking could freeze the Indian there.

Big as life, Marlboro Man. He drove right into the cross hairs, zooming larger into focus. Frampton, undercover cop. Follet's inside man.

White Bear knew the rifle was empty. The man was no fool. A drunk, maybe, but being hung over made him dangerous. A drunk's misery made various kinds of outrageous acts possible. Boyd suddenly felt stupid crouched behind the rock. He would do something bold and impenetrable, something he couldn't recover from. He stood up.

"Frampton," he called, waving the rifle above his head. As he approached he could not see his feet for the low-lying fog. He felt his legs cut through it, dividing it, clumping it into shapes. "I've come to ride with you."

Frampton looked him over. "Who're you?"

"Cubit's the name. You need wranglers to get these head upstream, and I can do just that."

"Cubit, huh? Who sent you?"

"I represent D. W. Ling," said Boyd. He produced Jennifer's envelope with the North Star brand. "Let's say I'm watchful of his interests."

Frampton glanced at the paper. "What interests?"

"Horseflesh, sir. And the welfare of his son."

Frampton's eyes narrowed. "You mean the Chinaman?"

"Uh-huh."

Frampton stopped chewing and spat.

Boyd looked up and scanned the weather. This cowboy was dumber than he looked. "Yep," he said, punching his gloved hands. "Storm's coming."

"Where's your horse?" asked Frampton.

"Over yonder."

Frampton looked around until he spotted the kid hanging in the tree. He shook his head, then pulled his Stetson down over his ears. "Well, let's ride."

They each walked off like it were a duel, Frampton to his snow machine, the wrangler and the Indian into the trees. Boyd found Adrian on her horse with a blanket around her and a stocking cap pulled over her head. On the ground in front of her was a mound of canvas tarpaulin. When he peeled it back he found the two braves seated back to back, bound and gagged.

"What do we do with them?" she asked.

Boyd turned to White Bear. "They're with you," he said. "Will they ride?"

White Bear looked offended. "They'll ride," he said.

Boyd tossed him his knife. "Cut 'em loose," he ordered.

White Bear cut the deer bindings and slid the carcass from the horse. Boyd turned to Adrian. "Don't ride with us," he said. "Frampton's gone on ahead and I'm sure he'll be waiting."

"What do you want me to do?"

"Stay in the rear and keep an eye on our friends. When I drop back, fall out and circle on ahead."

"What then?"

"Either Frampton joins the drive or he's fixing an ambush."

"If it's an ambush?"

"Get him."

Adrian watched him and pulled the blanket from her mouth.

"You better load this," he said, tossing her the rifle.

She handed him Jennifer's revolver and rode out. Next the Indians mounted up, White Bear on the kid's dappled gray, a small horse sagging under the man's weight. Boyd watched them enter the corral and round up the herd, the men hooting and whistling, almost innocent.

Soon a rumble went up and within minutes they had the herd separated and moving north. Boyd rode one perimeter, rope waving and yelling. He was Charlie Siringo now, writer and Pinkerton crazy. You had to be crazy to get your man. "Haagh!" he cried.

They tore out of the trees like a batch of crows and raced across open hills, dipping, then heaving up again into clouds of powder and hard breathing. They're crazy, he thought. They were intent on losing him. "Whoa," he said.

It didn't take long for the herd to rumble out of sight. Frampton, White Bear, and the others would be waiting for him at North Star, he thought. No sign of Adrian or Bud. She knew better than to run her horse full out over snow like that. He sat on the ground with Bronco standing loosely behind him. From up there the bare hills stretched away into a vague pinkness, gray and white up close but pink farther out. The sky vaulted with shafts, corridors. Somewhere in the world it was spring.

Two thousand feet higher, he thought, lighting a cigarette, *his* cigarette. It was a means of waiting. For what? he wondered. He listened to it gasp when it struck the snow. He took a deep breath and waited. It didn't feel like amputating a leg. Adrian had once told him that Shoshone woman once honored their dead by chopping off joints of their own fingers and burying the pieces. A shedding.

Inspired, he emptied the pack and propped each cigarette in a circle like twigs for a fire. Then he reached into his saddle bags for the rest of the carton and planted them. He lit the pile and watched it burn. Another part of his life up in smoke, he thought. He lay sprawled on the snow staring up at the sky, snow falling in his eyes. At the top of the world ghosts were coming down in elevators. They attended the high trails and moved in animal time. They felt the earth heave like herds, heard it gurgle like a deer with its lungs blood-filled.

For an instant there wasn't a sound, not even the wind, when it struck him why he'd come. The case had become a mission. It meant welding spirit to world, to cement the two, to infuse words with a slashing sense of wildness, its steamy entrails, buffalo and horse. To interpret the sky and to grow hair. To die a little. To continue breathing.

Soon Adrian appeared on the next hill with the pack horse in tow, approaching slowly, resolutely.

Bird woman.

When she got close she did not slow down. Her salute was neither military nor affectionate, but clean, beast-to-beast. She rode on.

A pink light spread out on the snow, lodging shadows behind the rocks. In the west the sun clotted among the clouds, gonging in the gods halfway around the world. Life was a monkey, all right, a wild horse. And now the horse wore a snowy mustache and grazed on a nameless bare hill.

Adrian had long since disappeared into the woods when he heard the shot. Somebody was always doing that—shooting at ghosts or revving an engine, revving good and loud, or felling with a chain saw a giant pine to brew a lousy cup of coffee, or wrapping himself with radio blast to keep out the night, or killing someone that you loved. It didn't matter because ghosts climbed into the music, into the saw blade, right down the bore. Ghosts hovered over horse shit, they clung to the grass. Up here you could hear yourself go crazy.

It was another half-hour before he came to the dead horse. It lay in a gully with its throat cut. He noticed its broken foreleg sunk down in the snow, the jagged bone. The force of the body falling had smashed its leg. Adrian had found it first. She had used a knife to put it out of its misery. She would hunt the man who did this, who couldn't even fix a dying horse with a bullet. In matters of horses, Adrian got even.

The snow stopped and the air clenched into a deep freeze. He could hear it in the leather. He rode into pine woods thick with windfall. Frost hung from the trees and scraped in the silence. The herd had been there, all right, the wide trail of their tracks slashing everything. When it got dark the horse led the way. "Follow the horses," Boyd whispered.

When at last he came out of the trees there was not a speck of daylight. The sky glistened like crystal. There stood Horse Chestnut, Rusty's bald-face mare, her eyes glowing like moons. Beside her, her foal. "Horse Chestnut, share," said Boyd.

Mother and foal turned into the woods.

North Star hung in the air at the end of a long valley. The valley was fenced and filled with horses steaming in the holding pens. The herds spread under the starry sky like a huge shadow over the snowy ground. Beyond the horses and set between sloping hillocks was the lodge. The property glittered with blue landing lights. Beside the main house was a barn and several outbuildings, the whole works enclosed with hurricane fencing adorned with concertina wire. It looked like the state pen at Rawlins.

Rich bastards, he thought. It wasn't the money that bothered him; it was their laziness when it came to quality. Quality to them was all wrapped up in names—straight bourbon, silver-tipped alligator boots, and the Winchester over the fireplace.

"You're a snob," Adrian had said. "That's what you are."

He saw the whole operation—from Paulos to White Bear to the governor—as a house of cards. The *New York Times*, heroin, Hollywood, and Chinese food, ditto. It was the world. And he was one of them, human, vain and power-mad.

Jennifer's pickup was parked in front of the big house. He tied Bronco to a tree and crouched behind the truck. He slipped in from the driver's side and felt under the dash. The heroin was gone. Somebody was beating him to the draw. Somebody with all the answers. Somebody who could work out in the open.

Just then the porch lit up. The gate rattled, then footsteps. Boyd eased himself to the ground and crawled under the truck. He lay watching a set of pearl-colored boots circle to the driver's side and get in. In a second the engine revved. Boyd lowered his head and prayed.

When he looked up he was alone under the stars. From the darkness a car horn wailed. He jumped to his feet and lunged for the gate. All at once a dog went into a nervous breakdown on the porch. It was no use running. He clasped the fence and stared into a flashlight the size of a flood lamp.

"Sherman." The voice came from the trees. Just then the dog leapt dragging a piece of chain. When he hit the other side of the gate the entire fence shook. His eyes bulged right out of his head, the look of a killer, the look you see in successful men. He was a Doberman, a shiny black coat that fit bone and sinew like a glove. With his head tilted back he looked like a snake, jets of steam through clenched fangs.

Just as the holder of the flashlight came into view, there was a beating overhead. Suddenly the snow thrust outward like a huge explosion, whipping Boyd's face. He could not see the chopper. He could make out nothing but light and the weird slow-motion shadows of the blades.

"Put down the gun," said God. "Repeat, put down the gun and no harm will come to you."

Boyd hesitated. It wasn't the words but the bullhorn, its authority. Cops and crooks alike, they both had it. Then he did something stupid. He fired at the chopper.

He knew it right away. He dropped the gun and threw up his hands. Swaying with his hands above his head made him feel stupid. "Okay," he shouted. "Okay, okay."

Out of nowhere a ghost appeared. Boyd sensed it was somebody he knew, someone he trusted. He lowered his hands.

The ghost hit him. He waited a second before giving himself over to it. It was like a cold snap. First there was heat and then the noise stopped altogether. He smiled, a child again, beyond sorrow.

When he came to, he lay strapped to a stretcher and he could move his front teeth. Adrian was pouring something scalding into him. "You really bleed," she said.

He blinked to settle things in focus. Men talking, the scratch of a radio, a woman's voice. "Over," it said. That was all. He closed his eyes.

"Boyd Sherman?"

When he looked it was the ugliest man in the world. Maciosek. Maciosek had a face full of flak and a wandering glass eye. "I'm Lieutenant Maciosek. Can you hear me?"

Adrian looked down on Boyd as if he were an accident,

something she felt responsible for and had to explain. "He can hear you," she said.

"Do you wish to make a statement?"

"Well," said Boyd, "I quit smoking."

Maciosek nodded. "Excuse me," he said, and left.

Enter, Follet.

"Hey Kimosabe, how we doing?"

Bundled in sheepskin, the chief squatted beside the stretcher and grinned. He assumed control. Follet felt most in control during a big operation. He ordered Adrian to the wagon for questioning and inspected Boyd's jaw.

"We'll get you some medical attention and you'll be shipshape."

Something was wrong, all right. When Everett Follet resorted to cliché, he was tense.

"Where am I?" asked Boyd.

"Laying on the ground looking at me. We're in a peck of trouble."

When Follet said *we're* in a peck of trouble that could only mean *you're* in a peck of trouble. "Sorry to have to do this, buddy. You have the right to remain silent."

Peck of trouble.

"What's the charge?"

"How about the murder of Al Ling, for starters?"

Boyd tried getting up. "Al Ling?" he said incredulously. "Chief, that's crazy."

Follet stared at him and shrugged. For a second he looked just like he did back in his office the day Boyd showed him the North Star brand on Jennifer's envelope. In a professional blink of an eye he'd become a stranger.

Boyd shut his eyes and took a deep breath. "So what am I supposed to do?" he asked.

"Get a lawyer."

Again Boyd tried getting up. Quickly, he began recounting

the events of that afternoon when Follet interrupted. "Where's your client?" he demanded.

Boyd lay back on the stretcher. "Hell if I know."

"You were supposed to protect her."

"I was hired to find her husband, remember?"

"Yeah," said the chief. "And I suspect she did everything but squeeze the trigger."

"What's that supposed to mean?"

"Hell, I don't know. I'm trying to round up rustlers. What are you trying to do?"

"You haven't got a motive."

"We got Ling's body and we got a match on the weapon. You know that forty-four you were waving out there?"

"That's Jennifer's."

"It's what killed Rusty Landrus," said Follet. "As for a motive, you tell us. You've been screwing the missus, Boyd."

Boyd suddenly felt overcome, as if he'd just been sprayed with buckshot. "Is my wife being charged?" he asked.

"I don't know yet. Tell me what I need and I'll know something."

"She didn't know anything about it."

"Convince me."

So that was it, thought Boyd. Follet had let him roam for a long time. Only now did the chief decide to pull the string. Follet was playing a very cagey endgame. He could not afford a draw. Bust Boyd Sherman for murder. Charge his wife.

Follet was called away to the radio. Later, a chopper landed and soon left again. Boyd watched its lights sink out of sight. Then there was Adrian, standing dazed with her hands in her pockets. Boyd tried raising his hands. "Where are we?" he asked.

"Montana."

"Montana? Isn't that a little strange?"

She nodded. "The chief's nervous about getting out of here."

"What did you tell them?"

"Everything," she said.

He tried recalling what *everything* meant as if it were an airtight seal on a can of snouse. There was nothing like being charged with murder to bring you down to earth.

"Who says I killed Ling?" he asked.

"Lieutenant Frampton," she said.

Boyd struggled against the restraints. "It's Lieutenant Frampton, Adrian, who's behind all this. *He* killed Ling. He's crooked. He's on the take."

Adrian stared at Boyd and puckered her lips in deep thought. She blinked. Then two detectives came and led her away. She whistled for Bud and was taken to a van. In seconds she was gone. Boyd shut his eyes to the stars. It was really happening, he thought.

Finally a convoy of wagons came curling down the moonlit ridge. Follet hollered for somebody to radio the rigs and order them to cut their flashers, where'd they think they were, Times Square?

The wagons pulled up in a row inside the perimeter of sheriff's outfits, disgorging detectives with shotguns. Follet shook hands with Maciosek and climbed aboard the next chopper.

Follet was gone. For the record he was never there.

Boyd lay so long on his back swallowing blood that he felt like throwing up. He began deep-breathing. Then he stopped. He stopped breathing altogether to hear something familiar.

Frampton was behind the land rover talking to Maciosek. Maciosek was Narcotics. It was Frampton who'd called the chopper on Boyd. And now Frampton stood over him, grinning. "You're already dead," he said.

The last thing Boyd saw was Frampton's face as the cop drew the blanket up over his head.

FIFTEEN

▼▼▼▼▼ IT WAS THE CRASH of steel that woke him. He opened his eyes and there was light—a hundred-watt bulb masked with chicken wire. Wall, sink, commode, a steel cot and an army blanket. The place smelled of plumbing.

In his sleep he'd been riding the Circle Bar in the rain. There was no Billy or Susie. An old Indian had whispered to him the terrible methods Uncle Luke had employed in acquiring the land. Boyd couldn't recall exactly where in the dream it had happened, but he was sure of it. Everybody had secrets about the way they came by things—land, wealth, women. What was not so secret was how we lost them. We lost them by waking up.

"Boyd Sherman?"

Boyd set his feet on the floor, wrapped himself in the blanket, and stood up. His face throbbed. At least five stitches battened his upper lip. "Who hit me?" he asked.

The guard slapped on the handcuffs and chuckled. "You don't know who hit you? Ol' Papa Bear hisself."

Boyd stepped out the door in jailhouse clothes. Starchy blue top and bottom, "Med. Dog PD" on the breast pocket. That's when his pants fell down.

"Get moving."

"Where to?"

"You'll see."

The door slammed and the guard followed him down the hall. To the left ran a long row of empty cells. On the right was an opaque glass window with vents through which he could make out the County Court Building.

At the end of the hall were the occupied cells. He recognized White Bear and the others. They lay around in faded blue outfits, snoozing. In the blur of the bars it looked like Custer's Last Stand.

Kyle White Bear lay on his cot with his feet on the wall. His face was swollen. "Hey, Cowboy, got a cigarette?"

No cigarette. Instead, a smell of sage so thick it seemed to tint the air. Boyd took long slow draughts of it. Despite the pain he was actually content. Then the door slammed and the sage broke off like someone'd just cut off his nose.

Instead of light bulbs the ceiling began tracking long fluorescent tubes, down one thin corridor, a hard right at the Coke machine, then left. Fluorescent lighting was evil, perpetrated by the Rand Corporation to level out psychic transmissions in the workplace. Increase productivity by chilling the synapses. Fluorescence encouraged methodology, its effects neurological, like filing the human force field under an electron scanner. It made you sluggish, beat you into a kind of air ventilation. And there were never any windows. No wonder cops didn't catch crooks anymore; they stored information.

Here was silicon silence. On two sides cops sat hunched in tiny cubicles punching data onto screens blinking with radioactive green columns. Computer keys made that blank plastic sound that said nothing was happening. Everything soft touch, carpeted floors, and the sci-fi tingle of phones.

"Wait here," said the guard. He knocked on Follet's door, entered, and closed it behind him. Boyd watched Linda the secretary ignore him. He'd been to Follet's office a hundred times. But now it was different, everything was different. It was embarrassing. He felt like he'd just been dropped by his bowling team or asked to give up his place in the pitching rotation. Nothing personal, just drop dead.

"Kimosabe."

The chief stretched back in his swivel chair with his hands behind his head. He wasn't exactly happy. "C'mon in here," he said.

When the cuffs came off, Boyd sat down.

"Sorry about the lip," said Follet.

Set up on the desk was a new chess game. Follet was black. "It's your move," he said.

Boyd stared at the board a long time before he moved. Standard opening.

Follet: Pawn to Queen four. "I suppose you know you're free," he said.

"I don't even know why I was held."

"We had to. It's a little something called probable cause." White move. "Where's my wife?"

"We're going to keep her," said Follet.

"On what?"

"Probable cause. Jennifer Landrus is still missing."

"Missing ain't dead, Chief."

"Your wife's a jealous woman," said Follet. Black move.

"My wife's a lot of things," said Boyd, "but jealous isn't one of them."

Follet winked. "What can you give me?"

"Chief, Frampton's a crook."

"No, no. You mean, Frampton's a cop."

"I mean Frampton's dealing from both sides of the deck." White Knight move.

125

"Well," said Follet, pushing a pawn, "I'll tell you. The thought has crossed my mind, yes it has. But I can't prove anything. I don't even have probable cause. And until I do it's better I keep my mouth shut."

"You don't have a wife looking at murder one."

"No, but you do."

White, move.

Boyd watched the chief capture his pawn. "What's that supposed to mean?"

Follet looked at him. "You're a private detective," he said. "You figure it out."

Boyd took a deep breath and touched his lip.

"Your move," said Follet.

Pawn takes pawn would leave his King exposed. Queen to Bishop three. Follet captures Knight.

White move, Queen captures pawn: check.

Follet began humming. He studied and hummed.

"Move, will ya?"

Queen to King two.

"Jesus," said Boyd. "All that time for that?"

"What's the matter with it?"

Boyd slammed the desk. "What the hell am I doing? Adrian's in jail, there's a murderer on the city payroll, and I'm playing chess."

"Hold on, tenderfoot."

White move.

Follet wanted to argue but saw a kill in the center of the board. Pawn take pawn.

White Bishop, move. Check.

Boyd decided to push. "Tell me about Frampton," he demanded.

"Good cop. Made lieutenant faster than anybody on this side of the Divide. Went undercover a year ago on this horse-rustling matter."

"And then?"

"He came up with some good leads. Promised to break it wide open . . ."

"Then it got too close to home," said Boyd. "Like Rusty Landrus."

Just then Follet upset the board, pieces flying everywhere. He looked like he'd just spilled his milk. "You got the floor," he said.

Boyd reached for a cigarette when he realized he'd quit. He took a deep breath.

"You got the murderer of Rusty Landrus," he said. "He sits across from you at every council meeting."

Chief leaned back with his hands behind his head. "Don't tell me—Clyde Paulos."

"Paulos snuffed Landrus because Landrus squealed on his horse-rustling scam. Besides that, he's bunking the wife."

Follet looked up from his belly. "We know," he said.

"Next, Mrs. Landrus hires me to find her husband. She really doesn't know it's a setup to frame me for the death of her husband."

"You give her a lot of credit," said Follet.

"All I know is, I was supposed to be found dead up in the mountains with the gun that did Landrus. That would clear everyone. Only one hitch: the hit lady reneged."

"And?"

"Clyde took her out."

"Clyde never left his restaurant."

"Frampton, Chief, remember? Your man in the mountains? He got Jennifer. And he murdered Al Ling."

"How do you know that?"

"White Bear told me."

Follet swiveled gently in his chair. He was thinking.

"So how far does this horse business go?" he asked.

Boyd shrugged. "You tell me. Landrus knew a man named Manetti."

"Manetti?"

Follet turned around in his chair so that he now faced the wall. Boyd started in about Max Cubit's involvement with bad company in the Midwest when he was interrupted.

"You know what happened up there yesterday?" said Follet. "I mobilize everybody, I alert the sheriff, and what do we get? A couple Indians and a corral full of horses nobody ever heard of. We got Montana's feathers so ruffled they're going to sue. Here the governor is threatening to sue the department and Paulos wants my badge. I'm seriously thinking of moving back to my wife's people in Idaho."

"They can't do that," said Boyd.

Follet swung around and faced Boyd. "They sure can, my friend. Mayor Sally's called an emergency meeting of the council for tonight. You know what that means? She's going to demand my resignation."

Boyd stared at the overturned chess pieces. "What did happen up there?" he asked.

Chief held out his hands. "Who knows?" he said. "We moved into position and when we went in it was too late. We didn't know it was Montana."

"You were out of your territory."

"That's true. But if you stay in this line of work very long you'll learn you've got to play your hunches. In the end it's all you got. By the way, thanks for White Bear."

"You get anything out of him?"

Follet blinked, barely shaking his head. "I don't think there's much to tell."

There was a knock at the door and the same patrolman entered. He was holding a shopping bag at arm's length. Follet motioned for him to hand it over. "My god, whaddya got in there?"

Boyd took the bag and pulled out his clothing. They were matted with vomit. "They didn't wash them," he said.

"Damn," said Follet. "Put those things back."

Boyd tore into the manila envelope containing his belongings. There was a wallet and a damp wad of hundred-dollar bills. "Better count it," said Follet.

When he finished counting it was close to ten thousand.

"Is it all there?"

"I don't know," said Boyd. "I never counted it before."

"You wouldn't mind explaining where you got it, would you, Kimosabe?"

"Client's fee."

"Client's fee? You mean stud fee, don't you?"

Boyd hitched his pants. When Follet saw he wasn't going to get an argument, he waved his hand. "Get out of here," he said.

Boyd changed his clothes and walked with the guard past the windows to the end of the block. "White Bear," he called.

The Indian sat on his cot with his feet up off the floor. His socks had no toes left. He looked up and blinked like he was coming to. "Cowboy," he said.

"I wanted to say good-bye."

White Bear walked to the bars. "You getting out? Sure, you're getting out. You didn't do nothing."

He smelled of cheap wine and dirt.

"I don't have any cigarettes," said Boyd. "I quit."

"You quit? That's too bad."

"Sorry. Listen, I gotta ask you something. It's about my wife."

"Your wife? What's her name?"

"Adrian. She's in jail."

"Jail, huh? That's too bad. She's one fine woman you got. She's a fighter. There's nothing happened up there. You can believe that. Me and my brothers, we was having fun, that's all. We tried putting the kid on her but she beat him good. She's a fighter, boy. You treat her good she'll bring you luck. She knows horses."

Boyd nodded. "Thanks," he said. He would buy the man some cigarettes.

At the front desk he signed himself out and asked about Adrian. Linda wouldn't look at him. "I'm sorry," she said. "I have no way of knowing that. You'll have to call women's detention."

Only some women could be that cold, he thought. They looked you straight in the eye and swore they never saw you before. Men were shamefaced; when they looked at you, you saw the gravity of their sin. Men pleaded for forgiveness even though they'd never manage to forgive themselves.

He stood on the station steps feeling the rain on his face like angel's breath, lightly, whispering in the budding trees, the street steaming and creasing like gift wrapping whenever a car passed. Spring had come to Medicine Dog.

On his way home he bought a paper. MAYOR DENOUNCES POLICE ACTION, it said. It went on about the Montana operation, citing officers Maciosek and Frampton. It mentioned horses once, heroin not at all. The slant was Follet's heavy-handed policies in pursuing crooks, that this was the umpteenth such instance over the years and that city council was in an uproar. Emergency meeting set for tonight.

Back at the trailer he searched the kitchen for coffee but found none. That's when he kicked over the dog dish. In his office dog shit pocked every level place in the room. It lay on the rug, his cot, even the top of his desk. "Buck," he called.

He entered United Way to thank Laura for feeding his dog. Finding her office empty, he decided to call Vern Chessley. He thought it was a good idea. He didn't really want to talk to the old man, but he liked the idea of having done it. He sat at the desk listening to the warble in the receiver, and watched the room grow dark.

"Hello, Vern?"

The old man sounded under the weather, like he'd just come up from some barbiturate sleep, or had lain in sheep dip for days and barely crawled out when he heard the phone ringing. "Who is this?" he rasped.

"This is Boyd."

"Who?"

"Boyd Sherman. I'm calling about Adrian."

"She ain't here."

"Yes, I know. She's in jail. She's in County Detention. She wants to see you."

"She wants to see me?"

"Yes. She's in the County Detention building. She wants to see you but you have to call and get your name on their list."

"Call?"

"Yes, you have to call them. She wants to see you. She needs your help. Good-bye."

When he hung up he spotted Buck standing against the desk. He reached down to pet him and instantly drew back his hand. Rigor mortis. The dog had tipped over like a frayed windup toy.

SIXTEEN

▼▼▼▼▼ AFTER FASHIONING A COFFIN from an old shoebox, Boyd went outside and dug a grave beneath the cottonwood in back of the trailer. He dug by the light of his office window. When he finished he set the shoebox into the three-foot hole and tossed some dirt.

"God," he prayed. That's all, just God.

He listened to the trains coupling in the yard across the street, then he heard his stomach growl. He quickly changed his clothes and took off down Railroad on his bicycle. The lights were on in town and the last of the shift-change traffic was over. It felt good to be back. The air swept over him smelling of sage. Sage was the promise of a life that made sense. Sage was being everywhere at once. Headlights, sage, and rattlesnake—a long summer, a convertible, and a ballgame on the radio. Breathing free.

At the Happy Trails Boyd ordered Chinese and read the paper. A month into the baseball season and no surprises in the standings. In the "Leisure" section a rock star was pleased with motherhood but wanted to resume her career as soon as possible.

Doloras again. He folded his paper convinced that the greatest feeling in the world was anonymity and ten thousand dollars. "Horse chestnuts," he said.

When Doloras smiled her face shifted like geologic plates. "Horse chestnuts?"

People were gutsy, all right. Just hanging in there. Like standing in against a flame thrower who didn't give a damn about anything except making you look stupid on three pitches. Jesus, what a life: four lanes of headlines and women, laserlike coast-to-coast. And now it was this town, this woman, and this cup of coffee.

"Horse chestnut share."

"Oh, you mean water chestnut. You don't mean horse—"

"Doloras, one night last winter I called about ten o'clock and ordered food to go. A lady arrived a short time later and picked it up. She paid for it."

"I don't know, Mr. Boyd."

"She was Jennifer Landrus and I think you knew her."

Doloras began waving her hands like she was covered with ants. "She come here, yes."

"Drugs, wasn't it?"

"Pardon me? Pardon me?"

"Horse. You use it. When I called last winter, you mistook me for someone else."

Before she could deny it he grabbed her and pushed up her sleeve. When she wrenched free she spilled a glass of water. "You pay now," she said.

"First you introduce me to Mr. Ling."

"Mr. Ling not here."

"He comes here to eat, I've seen him. He's back in the office and you're going to introduce me."

"I can't."

"Yes, you can. Unless you want trouble."

"Trouble, no."

He rose from the table and led her behind the counter, down a hallway past the restrooms, finally through swinging doors into the kitchen. "Go on," he urged.

Doloras spoke Chinese to the cook and entered the office. The cook was covered in clean sweat. It ran from his crew cut down over his face in sheets. He stared at Boyd and slung his ladle on a large steamy pot. Next he dried his face, then pulled a gun. "Turn around," he ordered.

Boyd turned and let the man frisk him. It was always too hot in the proverbial kitchen, he thought. Cooking was too intense for diners. People paid not to see, and this cook looked perfectly capable of hawking in the wonton.

Doloras came out and held the door for him. She was smiling. When the door closed behind him she was gone.

D. W. Ling was a skinny old geezer with lined elephant skin who wore a gray suit about three sizes too big. His silver hair was combed straight back and curled up over his collar. His watch slid loosely over the bone.

Right now Mr. Ling was eating. Whatever it was he held between his chopsticks it looked blue under the fluorescent light. When it disappeared in the man's mouth it sounded dry, like clucking way back in the throat. All you could hear in the room was the kitchen fan and the fierce breathing of the old man as he chewed.

"Mr. Sherman, I've been waiting to meet you."

"Same here," said Boyd.

"Please sit down. What would you like?"

"Thanks, I just finished dinner."

"Did you find it satisfactory?"

"Yes, excellent."

"I come here often for the chicken hearts," said Ling. "Only Doloras knows not to overcook them."

"They look delicious," said Boyd.

"Would you like one? Here, try it."

Ling dropped one into his saucer and pushed it toward Boyd. The private detective held it between his fingers studying it. Boyd Sherman, who could never even stand gizzards, plopped the heart into his mouth like it were a breath mint. The Chinaman watched him bite into it. "It's good, yes?"

Boyd felt the organ crush between his molars and his mouth fill with saliva. "It's good," he said.

The old man smiled, his facial lines stretching to form a perfect oval. His front teeth were capped and their gold rims peeked out. When he nodded he bent from the waist.

"Now," he said, resuming his eating, "what can I do for you?"

"First," said Boyd, "I want to express my condolences. I saw your nephew's body up at North Star."

"Thank you. Tell me, how did he die?"

"Murdered, sir. Shot in the heart with a forty-four automatic."

"Yes, I understand, but how did it happen?"

"I believe it was someone close. Someone who knew him."

"You mean Lieutenant Frampton. Let's not waste time, Mr. Sherman, I am a businessman. I regret to say that at first I had no idea Frampton was a detective. Which brings me to the reason why my nephew was up there in that ridiculous outfit in the first place."

He dabbed his lips with an embroidered napkin and sipped coffee. When he looked up he was dead serious. "My nephew was delivering stolen horses, Mr. Sherman. You know that, of course, you're a private investigator. But do you know why?"

"Drugs?"

Ling smiled. "Heavens, no," he said, almost embarrassed.

"I get the feeling you're about to tell me," said Boyd.

"You're a good detective, Mr. Sherman. But you would never learn my reasons unless I told you."

He offered Boyd a cigarette, was waved off, then fit one into an ivory holder and lit up. "And, I might add, nothing that is spoken in this room will be repeated."

At which Boyd raised his eyebrows.

"You see, Mr. Sherman, I trust you."

It was hard to tell if that was a compliment or a warning. "Go on," said Boyd.

Ling put his elbows on the table. When he exhaled he puckered and produced little bursts of smoke. "North Star is my operation," he said. "You're familiar with it, I believe? It's a holding company, so to speak. And despite its dealings with the kind of people who would murder my nephew, its purpose is and always has been open trade with China."

Boyd grinned. "China needs horses?"

"China wants horse meat."

"They eat it?"

"They sell it to Japan."

"At a hefty profit, I suppose."

"Quite profitable. Are you interested?"

"Some other time."

Ling sat back and squinted through the smoke. "Are you familiar with the history of my people, Mr. Sherman?"

"More or less."

"The first horse came from China, did you know that?"

"Not exactly."

"He's called the dawn horse and dates back a million years. He was no bigger than twenty inches high and had four toes on his front feet."

"Medicine dog."

"From him evolved others, the *Orohippus* and the *Epihippus*, followed by the *Mesohippus* and, much later, the *Merychippus*

137

or Miocene horse. They say he was the size of a Shetland pony. You can find their remains all over Wyoming."

"I'm impressed."

"When I embark upon a project I like to know what I'm dealing with."

"I see."

"Mr. Sherman, permit me to ask. Do you know what you're dealing with?"

"I think you and I measure success a little differently," said Boyd.

"Tell me, how do you measure it?"

"I survive and collect my fee. That allows me to think what I want."

"Independent," said Ling.

"Not really. Women mess me up. Sit twenty of them at the bar and I'll pick the sickest one every time."

"Ha, the sickest one, ha ha. There's much to be said for arranged marriages."

"Like Rusty and Jennifer Landrus?"

Ling shook his head. "It's too bad about them," he said. "A nasty business. It's that Greek."

"Paulos?"

"And Lieutenant Frampton. In a state with a smaller population than most counties in California, everybody knows a bad cop, Mr. Sherman. That is everybody but Chief Follet."

"Who murdered Rusty?"

Ling cocked an eyebrow. "Hard to say."

"No, it's not. Which one, the cop or the cowboy?"

Ling crushed his cigarette. "Cops, cowboys, what's the difference?"

"Look, I'll say cop and you light another cigarette. If it's the cowboy don't do anything."

"What if it's neither?"

"Then keep doing nothing. Ready? Frampton."

The old man lit a cigarette.

"But Paulos knew about it."

Ling removed another cigarette, lit it off the one in his holder, and offered it. Boyd took it, held it under his nose, and stubbed it out.

"What about Mrs. Landrus?"

"Who can say? You see, that was never supposed to happen. Mr. Landrus became dangerous to the Greek when he noticed irregularities in the local stable operations."

"Like stealing good horses."

"Unfortunately."

"Why did you have Mrs. Landrus's horses stolen?"

"To get your attention. I wanted Lieutenant Frampton out of the way. He was taking my profits."

"Instead you lost a nephew."

"I'll tell you something about my people," said Ling. "As long as the trains ran and it required coal to feed them, the Chinese belonged here. We had just arrived when the Union Pacific used us against its own people. We were used to break the will of the workers. A hundred years ago the Americans came into Chinatown after us, not to set an example but to obliterate us. On that day my grandfather was shot and left to die in Bitter Creek. I can show you the spot if you like. My family could not stand still to mourn. They were loaded into boxcars and taken to Evanston. They taught me about grief and what steps needed to be taken. In war, Mr. Sherman, both sides must expect losses."

Boyd stared at the old man. He had no quarrel with him. The old man had probably never even heard of Chuang Tzu.

"Get this Frampton," said Ling with quiet yet granite intensity.

Boyd nodded. "How's Frampton fit into North Star?" he asked.

"*I* am North Star," said Ling. "The politicians took the name for their ranch, that's all. They take orders from me. They get their percentage. Frampton is their man. The Greek is their man. The Landruses were theirs. The Greek oversees the operation up there. He got greedy, that's all. He called in the wop from Nevada and started skimming the herd, first rustling a lot of good horses, mixing them with our mustangs and then selling them off for saddle horses. I suspect that's what my nephew discovered when they killed him."

"Paulos's man in Nevada, is it Manetti?"

"Yes, Manetti."

"He's Mafia."

Ling smiled.

Boyd watched him a second. Of course, he thought. Ling was an old tong godfather. The Triad, the Chinese Mafia, was dealing horses out of Hong Kong. It was not a good idea to ask. Unlike Max Cubit, this man was not a drunken psychopath craving a sense of self-importance. This man ate dinner in Medicine Dog, Wyoming, but that didn't mean he was small change. This man could arrange things.

"So what are you going to do?"

"Nothing," said Ling. "I'll wait. Go for a walk."

The old man got up from the table and fished in his pocket for a tip. "I would ask you to accompany me," he said, "but I don't think that would be wise in light of what you know."

Boyd rose and opened the door. "After you," he said.

Boyd followed the old man through the kitchen into the dining room. Ling stopped and spoke to Doloras while Boyd sat at the bar and peeled the paper off a toothpick. Soon Doloras came over smiling, in her hand a double whiskey. "Mr. Ling say you look like whiskey man." She set it down in front of him and put her hands on her hips. "On the house," she said.

He could suddenly envision Doloras in a Chinese production of *Macbeth*. Hong Kong street theater. He felt a strong urge to give her money. He pushed the drink toward her. "You take it," he said.

"Naw, naw," she insisted, waving her finger.

It became deadly serious that he refuse the drink. It was the first drink that got you drunk, he thought. He had always known it would come down to this. "Thanks," he said.

He looked up from the drink and saw the *Stampede* girl, the cut-out kid from the Mustang. She was at a corner booth with Abe Marsh, the reverend himself. They were drinking.

Boyd looked at Doloras. "Hey, is that your dealer?" he asked.

Doloras began humming. "Who, that? Why? What you want to know for?"

Boyd pulled out a hundred dollars and set it on the bar.

"I never see him before," she said.

Boyd smiled. "Give me three dollars' worth of quarters," he said. "And bring me the gun from the cash register."

Her eyes suddenly sharpened into daggers. When she brought the money he left a two-dollar tip, picked up the double whiskey and the gun, and headed for the booth.

"Reverend Marsh, you ol' sonofagun. What brings you out this beautiful evening? Have a drink on me," he said, setting the double whiskey on the table.

The reverend looked a little shaken. "Beg your pardon?" he said.

Boyd slammed a fistful of quarters on the table. "Who's your pretty date, Reverend? Mind if I get her to play some music?"

Marsh swept the quarters onto the floor. "No music," he growled.

Boyd squatted to retrieve the money and saw Marsh's boots. They were the same pearl-colored jobs he'd seen under the truck at North Star. Then he saw something else. In the gloom he could make out the fat man's paw on the girl's thigh.

Boyd sat down beside the girl and put his arm around her. "Hi, remember me?"

Marsh fumbled with his zipper and sprang to his feet. "Don't you talk to this man. You don't have to say anything."

Boyd lay the quarters in the girl's hand and stood up. "Go ahead, Mary."

"Sue," she said.

Marsh next stuck his finger right in Boyd's face. "Mister, I'm warning you."

Boyd winked at the girl. "Play some music," he said.

She slid out of the booth and headed for the juke.

"Hey, just a minute," said Marsh.

Boyd grabbed the fat man by his bollo tie and shoved the gun in his gut. "I don't want you, Marsh, but you cross my path again and I'll let your air out. I'll have you up on statutory rape and contributing to the delinquency. And I'll make it stick. You got a record, Reverend. One more diddling with a minor and you'll be sniffing the boys in maximum."

Marsh was sweating. It smelled like cleaning fluids. "Whaddya want?" he asked.

"Paulos. He sent you up to the mountains—what for?"

"What?"

"North Star, *comprende?* You drove off in Landrus's pickup just before the bust."

Music boomed down like thunder. The reverend said something but all there was were his sweaty lips. Boyd tugged on the man's tie. "What?" he yelled.

The reverend began blathering about orders to punish Miss Jennifer. Paulos had instructed Jennifer to snuff her private eye, and when she failed in her mission he put out his contract.

When the song ended Marsh was shouting. "I never saw her," he said.

"Who's the girl?" Boyd demanded.

Marsh became ingratiating. "Just Paulos's niece, he said. "I can explain. Let's have a drink."

Boyd told the girl to get out of there. Just as she turned to leave, the reverend brought his knee up. All at once the table flipped, throwing drinks everywhere. In an instant Boyd was on the floor with pain shooting through his side. The gun was skidding across the floor. The next thing he saw was the table landing on him. He covered his head and heard glass breaking.

Boyd scrambled to the door. The last thing he heard was music and Doloras shouting. Outside, he saw headlights and a full moon. He heard two shots. If only the steps hadn't moved. He could not get them to come to him. He tugged on the railing to bring them up, to get his feet to them, but instead there was this enormous falling. He thought Doloras was pulling him backward. Then he felt something give. It was the door. When it closed again he lay on the top step tasting blood.

"I'm hit," he said.

Dragon lady was yanking his arm. "You're not hit," she said.

Boyd checked himself. She was right. It was a hairline cut over his right eyebrow.

In the headlights it was hard to see. For a moment no one appeared and then there were voices from behind a limousine. When he got up he saw D. W. Ling and his chauffeur approaching. Ling was lighting a cigarette and the chauffeur held a gun.

"Are you all right?" asked Ling.

"He's okay," said Doloras.

"It seems Lieutenant Frampton was trying to silence this gentleman," said Ling, pointing at Marsh. We must be on our way."

Reverend Marsh lay in his own blood. "Is he dead?" asked Boyd.

Ling didn't answer. "We've got the girl," he said. "She's fine."

"I'll take her," said Boyd.

The old man nodded. It was almost a bow. "As you wish," he said.

SEVENTEEN

▼▼▼▼ SHE WASN'T A BAD kid. At the Mustang she'd seemed stupid, but it was the drugs. It wasn't until they walked the five blocks to City Hall that he learned some things about Sue McDonald. That her parents had been killed in a head-on with an oil-field truck, that she'd once fallen for a guy named Bobby, and that she'd got pregnant and had an abortion. And that after a year in Worland reformatory for being picked up on possession of a bag of marijuana, she was brought back to Medicine Dog and court-ordered to attend high school and get a part-time job. Enter, Clyde Paulos, a "friend of the family."

Small western towns were incestuous, all right. It was the local cottage industry to reinvent the Jack Mormon by raising fine kids who later flipped out and made Mini-Mart cashiers lie face down on the floor begging please. It was different with wayward Catholics. A lapsed Catholic like Boyd was dark, moody, and interior. He pulled the blanket of original sin up over his head and played with himself. A Mormon gone astray cut a vein and let it splash in public places. It was the mountains, hard winters, and families tied together with barbed wire. Twenty years of that and you began shouting at God in your sleep. You held a shotgun on Him.

That explained Clyde Paulos, rodeo star and raconteur, Greek cuisine and horse shit.

"The bastard's Mormon?" exclaimed Boyd.

"A convert," said the girl. "So am I."

Somehow that changed everything. Boyd shook his head, lost for words. Butch Cassidy was Mormon, his grandfather a bishop. Who would have thought?

"But he's Greek!"

Sue McDonald shrugged.

She'd called him Uncle and worked long hours at the Mustang. Later he introduced her to Reverend Marsh, who'd introduced her to heroin and forcible sex.

"How'd you feel about that?" asked Boyd.

"Oh," she said, "not much."

"It doesn't bother you?"

"I don't know, I guess so."

"You're not going to see Uncle Clyde anymore."

He explained where they were going and how important it was that she cooperate. She was to testify to some things he was going to say about Paulos and then she wouldn't have to do what he said anymore. Did that sound okay?

She stopped dead in her tracks. "No," she said. "They'll put me back in Worland."

She wheeled and walked away.

"It'll be all right," he said, going after her. "I promise. We'll get you a place to stay. I won't let them send you back."

At City Hall he guided her up the steps while cars pulled up, discharging citizens for the meeting.

What exactly he was going to do, he wasn't sure. Mayor Crab's motion to dismiss the chief was probably first on the agenda. Quickly Boyd led his witness away from the traffic and waited in a ground-floor lounge. There he bought her coffee and showed her the ladies' room. "Wash your face," he said. "And do something about your hair."

He paced the windowless room, waiting. He tried sitting in one of the plastic chairs but it was no use. It bothered him to consider what he was about to do. But it meant getting Adrian out of jail. And who would he put in her place? A dead man, a cowboy, and a cop. The dead man he could make stick.

Next he weighed the cost. He had to nail Paulos or lose Sue McDonald. He had to talk fast and then let her testify. It was a gamble, and he wasn't just playing with his job. It meant saving himself.

At the coffee machine he read the buttons. Coffee black. Just then a hand passed over his right shoulder and inserted coins. Boyd felt the hair on his neck bristle. It was Frampton. Boyd turned so suddenly he spilled his coffee.

Frampton sucked air through his teeth as he rocked back and forth on his western heels, jingling change in his pocket. He looked like a man who'd let go of any moral compunction and now resided cooly in the idea that satisfaction was obtained merely by managing his life correctly. He exuded the slimy confidence of men with delusions.

"You going to the meeting?" asked Boyd.

Frampton nodded.

"What are they doing in there?"

Frampton drew a miniature cigar from his jacket and lit up. "Old business, I expect."

"How long'll that take?"

The lieutenant shrugged. "Who knows?"

Frampton resumed jingling his change. He was looking at a print on the wall, a landscape, of course. In Wyoming that was all they looked at. Pictures of rocks and portraits of game. You'd think they'd finally want something else, a splash of color, a burst of feeling not compressed into something viewed through binoculars or a gun sight.

Finally, Frampton turned to Boyd. "Seeing that we're asking questions, how come a wimp like you has such a capable woman?"

Boyd set down his cup. "What are you talking about?"

"Remember the Suburban at the funeral? That was me." Frampton shook his head and chuckled. "I chased you through the desert to see what you were made of. Instead, I find out what your wife's made of. She *is* still your wife, ain't she?"

Boyd reached for his coffee, then stopped. He was staring right into Frampton's eyes. "I know what you're doing," he said.

He ran to the ladies' room and knocked. When she didn't answer, he entered. "Susan?"

He saw her feet in the first stall. "You okay?" he asked. Again, no answer. He banged on the door.

Then he heard something hit the floor. When he fell to his hands and knees he saw it. It was a plastic disposable syringe. "Open up," he demanded.

When she didn't respond, he crawled underneath the door. She was seated on the toilet with her head tilted back. He clasped her shoulders and shook. "What are you doing?" he yelled.

He saw by the syringe that she hadn't taken all of it. All of it would have killed her. He helped her to her feet and led her to the sinks where he forced her to see herself in the mirror. "You see that?" he said. "That's a ghost. You're the walking dead, Susan. Do you want to die?"

He forced her head against the mirror. "Let go of me," she cried.

"Answer me, do you want to die?"

"Yes!" she said.

He turned her around and looked at her. Her eyes were

glazed like two lead bullets. "Okay," he said, "then you got nothing to lose."

He took her by the arm and nearly dragged her across the hall. Suddenly they were in the council chambers, in the very back. The room was strictly SRO with every conceivable stock of citizen angry and accounted for. He hadn't seen this big a turnout since the NRA came to town to make trouble. Guns and horses always got the people out.

Mayor Sally had the floor. She sat at a podium in her butterfly glasses talking into a microphone about police jurisdiction. The audience looked mean. Tonight they wanted Follet's ass on a platter.

When Boyd had fought his way to the front, he shouted, "Ladies and gentlemen."

Mayor Sally lowered her glasses while some bald-headed administrator grabbed the mike. "You're out of order, sir." A small commotion rippled through the crowd.

"Listen to me, Mayor."

"Sir?" said Baldy. "Sir, you're out . . ."

The crowd loved a troublemaker. "Let him say his piece," they said. "Go on, mister."

Finally, Mayor Sally cleared her throat. "What is your name, sir?"

"Boyd Sherman, private detective."

The crowd grumbled. Mayor Sally covered the mike and consulted with council members. Next she slammed the gavel and asked Boyd what his business with the council was.

"My business is with you, Mayor."

The crowd liked that.

Again Mayor Sally lowered the gavel. She looked like a schoolmarm facing revolt from her charges. "What item on the agenda have you come to address, Mr. Sherman?"

"Chief Follet's investigation of the horse rustling."

"What horse rustling?" yelled someone from the back. "You

mean the government conspiracy to kill off our mustangs, don't you?"

"You tell 'em, Virgil," someone yelled.

Again the gavel. "I will adjourn this meeting if I have to," warned the mayor. She instructed Boyd to take his place at the podium and address the council.

At that moment, Lieutenant Frampton entered through the council doors and whispered something to Councilman Paulos. Paulos covered his mike with a black hood, then excused himself to the mayor before following the lieutenant outside. Meanwhile, Boyd led his witness to the podium, then grabbed the microphone. "First of all, the chief's doing exactly what he's paid to do."

"Mr. Sherman," the mayor interrupted, "would you mind telling us who that person is you're with?"

"Her name's Sue McDonald."

"Is she all right?"

"She's not all right, Mayor. And I've brought her here to tell you her story. I think you'll find it . . ."

He paused to weigh the right word, to shape it like a round, load and fire. When he squeezed the trigger nothing happened. "Interesting," he said.

"She better be nineteen," yelled Baldy.

The crowd was getting nervous. Somebody yelled, "Look out!"

Sue McDonald was coming off the wall. Boyd turned and grabbed her, realizing at once that this was not the time to tell his story. Instead he would let his witness do the talking. She wouldn't last much longer.

"Mayor, members of the council, citizens of Medicine Dog, Miss McDonald is presently under the effects of heroin, a drug supplied to her by Mr. Clyde Paulos."

The place erupted. Gavel, Mayor Sally shouting, feedback

from the mike, and Baldy playing the electronics troubleshooter.

"This is not the police station," said the mayor.

"But the police station's on trial," said Boyd. "And once you hear Miss McDonald I believe many of your questions will be answered."

"Are you Sue McDonald?" asked the mayor.

Boyd's client thought about it a few seconds, then nodded vigorously.

"Yes, she is," said Boyd.

"I see," said the mayor. She began to write something.

The council broke into whispers. Suddenly a paunchy professional named Sloan broke the microphone silence. "Go ahead, Miss McDonald."

Sue kept batting something in front of her face. Whatever it was appeared to be sticking to her hands. It was the air. Finally she took the mike in both hands. "Well," she began. "Ah . . ." Then she began sobbing.

Boyd intervened. "Excuse me," he said, "but maybe it would be better if I asked her some questions."

He squeezed her arm. "Sue, tell these people how your parents died."

"They're, ah, dead," she said.

"How?"

"How?"

Boyd decided to switch strategies. It was like being ten points down in the final quarter, your zone defense had holes and it was time to go man-to-man. He'd ask the questions and she'd say yes or no. They would be leading questions. For the first time he knew for certain he'd missed his calling. I should have been a lawyer, he thought.

"They were killed together in a car accident five years ago. Is that right? Just nod your head."

She nodded.

"You were later awarded to Mr. Clyde Paulos's custody. Is that so?"

She didn't understand the question.

"Uncle Clyde took care of you."

When she smiled it made her whole face look hopeless.

"Just nod yes or no."

She nodded.

Boyd then proceeded to outline her life under the care of Paulos. Failure to ensure her education, the complete lack of moral guidance . . .

She laughed. "He guided me, all right," she said. She was running her fingers through her dirty hair.

"Could you explain?"

"He made me go with the reverend."

"You mean Abe Marsh."

She nodded. "Preacher Marsh got dressed up in rhinestone duds and called me into his room. Then he . . ."

"Then he what?"

"Well, no, that came after. First he gave me stuff."

"Stuff?"

She was struggling. "Clothes," she whined, "and a horse . . ."

"Drugs? Did he give you drugs?"

She nodded.

"And then he . . ."

"Called me into his room. I mean he'd make me. He'd make me take off my clothes."

The crowd sounded properly appalled. Before the mayor could find her gavel, however, Boyd pressed on.

"He'd make you take off your clothes and what?"

"Sit on his saddle."

"What?"

"Sit on his saddle, you know. He kept a saddle in his room. He'd lay on the bed and tell me how to move."

"Did he touch you?"

"Sometimes. He said he was teaching me stunts."

"What kind of stunts?"

"Cowgirl stunts. He said they were old, back before the white man. The Spanish ladies did them; they learned from the Indians."

For those not familiar with the reverend, Boyd explained about Marsh's relationship with Mr. Paulos. According to his witness, the sex came with the heroin. This went on for a year before Jennifer Landrus became Clyde's girlfriend. He'd got Jennifer going on the stuff.

"There was no sex between you and your uncle?"

"Not exactly."

"Explain that, please."

"Uncle Clyde liked to see women go at it."

"What?"

Mayor Sally looked anxious. "What is the point of all this?" she asked. But the locals shouted her down.

Sue was scratching her face. "He used to make me and Jenny get on his bed and . . . you know."

"While he watched."

"He'd get excited."

"And then?"

"Then he'd get on top of her."

"And what did you do?"

She thought about it for a second then shrugged. "I watched."

Mayor Sally slammed down the gavel. "I must intervene here, Mr. Sherman. Unless you can show us what this has to do with the item on the agenda . . ."

"Just this," said Boyd. "That Clyde Paulos was mixed up in

some high-level horse dealing. That his operation extended to Idaho, Utah, and Montana, and that his business associates have Italian last names and are counted among national high rollers. That—let me continue—Mr. Paulos was so prominent in various horse scams he became a threat to the competition. It was necessary for him to cement alliances. That required supplying clients with sex, drugs, and horseflesh."

It was here that Sue McDonald floated to the center of the room and dropped her pants. When she bent over, beaming from her right white cheek was a tattoo, or rather a brand. North Star. She waved it for the whole council to see before the detectives got to her. "Order in the chamber, order in the chamber," commanded Mayor Sally.

When some order was restored, Boyd regained the floor. "Among his clients," he continued, "was North Star Ranch, Wyoming."

More commotion in the chamber.

"Don't you see," he shouted, "Rusty Landrus was just a wrangler who got wise. That's why Paulos had him executed. And there's nobody better to carry out an execution than Lieutenant Frampton, Medicine Dog PD."

The crowd boomed like a big wind.

"That's right, Mayor. The murderer of Mr. and Mrs. Landrus."

Chief Follet had entered during the testimony and stood against the wall. When the noise subsided, Mayor Sally sipped water. "Glad to see you could make it," she said. She didn't look at Follet when she spoke.

The chief uncrossed his arms and grinned. "Please excuse my absence," he said, "but we had a call."

The mayor still refused to look at him. "Chief Follet, you have lots of calls. Why couldn't you send a detective?"

"I'd rather not say," he replied.

The mayor turned red. She snorted into the mike. "The item

on the agenda we're discussing is your performance on the job. I think it wise you tell us what's so important as to prevent you from attending."

Follet hitched his pants. "Mayor, you trying to tell me how to do my job?"

Before the mayor could respond, Baldy whispered something in her ear. Again the gavel. "It seems," she said, "that a homicide has been committed just a few minutes ago. The victim's been identified as Abraham Marsh, pastor."

"Now you understand why I couldn't send a detective?" said Follet.

The room went crazy while the mayor gaveled and Marsh's sister wailed like a professional mourner. Chief Follet grinned and shook his head. Boyd tapped the microphone. "Mayor, if I may continue."

It was no use. News of Paulos had spread through the crowd like a grass fire. Finally, somebody shouted, "Mayor, is it true Clyde Paulos just got arrested for drugs?"

Mayor Sally brought the room to order. "Chief Follet, is it true that Clyde Paulos has just been arrested for possession of narcotics?"

"Yes, Mayor, it is."

The Chief next turned to Boyd. "It's the only thing we could get him for," he said, resignedly.

In the heat of incoming information, the murder of Marsh and Paulos's bust added up to a big night on Main Street. Just then a woman entered riding Rusty Landrus's mare, Horse Chestnut. Folks cleared a path.

It was her, all right. Jennifer Landrus, client at large. She sat mounted center stage in tight-fitting buckskin pants and a fringed jacket, packing a six shooter on her hip. Detectives flanked her on all sides in a crouch, revolvers aimed.

She refused to identify herself to the council. She had just one thing to say. "Where's Clyde Paulos?" she demanded.

Pandemonium.

Boyd tapped the mike. "Mayor, if I may continue . . ."

It was no use. Mayor Sally hammered the desk to adjourn the meeting, but it was already over. Horse Chestnut reared, looking as spooked as ever. Jennifer got down and tried calming her, but it was no use. The mare's blue eyes were beacons of insanity. She started prancing in a circle, then kicked once like a rodeo bronc. Everybody pressed for the exits, overturning chairs and making a mess of the place. Sue McDonald was taken into protective custody by the detectives. They took her out through a private door that led directly into the police station. When Boyd insisted on going with her, they handcuffed him.

"What the hell?" he said.

The cop shoved him against the wall. Behind the tinted glasses his eyes were sharp with professional malice. "Listen to him," said his partner. "He's a tough guy now."

The cop with the glasses grabbed Boyd by the shirt. "Look, asshole," he said, "we was set to go in. We would have had them, not just a couple of Indians. Then you show up, wandering around with your finger up your ass. By the time chief took you out, some sonofabitch'd called the chopper."

"I didn't call that chopper," Boyd argued.

"I didn't say you called no chopper. You threw the timing way off, boy. You screwed the whole thing, so shut the fuck up!"

Boyd watched the man's trigger finger aimed right at his nose. He wanted to rant about Frampton, Manetti, the governor, everybody. He wanted to talk to his client.

But he didn't. He didn't say anything. Suddenly he decided it was better to do as the man said and shut the fuck up.

He wandered into an empty interrogation room listening to the calls come in from the patrols. He thought he recognized

Skeeter reporting in; just another day on the beat, he thought. He craved a cigarette.

Just then Chief Follet looked in. For a moment he and Boyd looked each other right in the eyes. Without saying a word, the big guy turned and headed down the hall. Just as Boyd reached the door to call him, Paulos appeared at the front desk with Maciosek. Paulos was emptying his pockets while some guy from the *Stampede* took his picture. "Hey, get outta here," yelled Maciosek.

Then followed shots—two at point-blank.

Boyd had seen it coming. For an instant he saw her, the familiar look of her face, the furtive look in her eyes. She remained someone between a stranger and a lover, someone—

Then it was too late. With the gun blast Paulos doubled over. Maciosek batted the gun from her while a patrolman wrestled her to the floor. Boyd held his cuffed hands out. "Jennifer!" he yelled.

When they picked her off the floor she blinked like she were coming to from a deep sleep. Tears streamed down her cheeks. She was smiling.

EIGHTEEN

▼▼▼▼▼ THE NATIVES SAID THERE were two seasons in Medicine Dog, winter and the Fourth of July.

It was the Fourth of July. By nine A.M. it was ninety and climbing. Rolling out of bed, Boyd couldn't remember sleeping.

The week's *Stampede* said hot; WIND radio—hot, with a chance of thundershowers in the early evening. On the river fishermen waded up to their shoulders and cast. Earlier that week Boyd had fished from a bridge, snagged a bush, and lost his hook. He'd spent that afternoon lying in the grass watching the eagles over Horseshoe Rock. Eagles mated for life, Adrian had said. Eagles and wolves and Canadian geese.

In the evenings he'd walk around checking out the company softball games going on under the lights. Adrian played third base for Wilderness. Last Tuesday, trailing 18–3, she'd stood in a perpetual crouch blowing gum and pounding her mitt while the visitors batted around and around. She'd never got to make a play. Sometimes in the middle innings he had felt a sudden warmth like a waft of popcorn or perfume, the soft breeze from right, like a cat purring. Adrian, softball, and the crawl of headlights beside the river. What could he say? He'd looked up beyond the lights at the stars.

The morning she was released from jail they went to her place and made love. It was the first truly hot day. They walked around the apartment naked, guzzling ice tea and listening to Spanish guitar on the stereo. Again, he imagined her life without him. He could not get to the bottom of it. They made love over and over through two shift changes and the sun setting. When they dressed they sat on the porch steps above the street talking to Bud and listening to the kids and the music and the men getting drunk.

"Are we going to get divorced or not?" she'd asked.

He didn't know, he'd said. But it occurred to him that maybe things would be different.

It was only when he was by himself that he knew for sure. And with ten thousand dollars and nothing to do, that meant basking in the slow routines that reminded him of growing up. It signaled middle age. The loose, slumping movement of his body through terrific heat, the somnolent attention to details, the blind hope of love. All teenage boys were private eyes, he thought. They played their hunches and they got lucky. But he had grown up reticent; suddenly there had been too much to lose. That was why it was right and fitting that he now made his living at private investigation.

Emblazoned on his T-shirt: BOYD SHERMAN INVESTIGATIONS. Next he'd get the baseball cap.

Out beyond the interstate, in the haze of cities, the world had grown too old. He was the last private eye. And in Medicine Dog they knew his name. Hell, that wasn't so bad.

It only scared him when he thought it was forever, when he imagined dying here, poked into the frozen earth, Adrian and a priest up on the hill, short and sweet, no big deal.

But that was exactly what Wyoming had impressed upon

him. That life was short with seeds of sweetness. Like summer, for instance, and a woman. And most of all that it was no big deal, a line of pickup trucks with their lights on, your name inscribed on a slab of stone.

Finally there was no place left to go. Welcome to Medicine Dog, population eight thousand more or less. Home of the Mustangs and an alumna named Adrian Chessley. Home of Boyd Sherman, private detective, "My card, ma'am."

Why, just the other day he'd received a homemade document in the mail. It said he was legally permitted to practice the demonic arts of private investigation within the town limits. Signed, Everett Follet, Chief of Police. Boyd thumbtacked it over the desk.

At ten o'clock Mike Hagar, DJ and raconteur, began the news. Boyd mopped his face with a washrag and tied his tie. In one hour he'd be sitting in the WIND studio fetching questions on "The A.M. Show." Hagar thought it a good idea. "Medicine Dog's own gumshoe," he'd announced. Hagar was very good at what he did. Maybe that said something about the business.

Boyd had agreed to the interview so long as they stayed away from the Landrus case. His client was in jail but that was no reason to talk about her as if she were dead.

In other news, Sue McDonald had disappeared for a while. After being dragged through the court, she'd faced a battery of social agencies trying to clean her up. She was now attending adult classes in hopes of obtaining a high school equivalency diploma. It probably wouldn't happen, but that was what it was all about. That was what he wanted to say on the radio. There were no happy endings but most of us managed.

He kept thinking about the brand on the girl's butt. We all belonged to somebody.

Anyway, he'd kept his promise. He'd found her a place to live at Vern Chessley's, way out of town with the sheep dip and the wind and the old lady's ghost whistling in the cracks of the house. The old man would give the kid a square deal and lay it out plainly on the table, and that was exactly what she needed. Why couldn't everybody manage that? Make an offer. Vern would give her a place in exchange for help with the chores and a chance of his being found when he dropped dead on the range.

And what could Boyd offer Adrian? As husband and wife, what could they do for each other? She was already back working double shifts at the mine. Tonight would be their first real date—ever. He'd meet her at the ballgame and they'd eat dinner at the Happy Trails. He'd tell her what Follet had said, that the chief was never serious about holding her, that the evidence didn't stack up. Follet had merely used her to get Boyd moving on the case. And besides, the old cop knew she didn't do it. Old cops knew those things.

And still there was Jennifer. Maybe he'd made her up, that despite all the evidence, he'd made her up to be just a wild kid who made him feel old. It was because he made things up that he could never be sure.

Ghosts again. He didn't know what else to call them. He was haunted and wondered if he didn't have something to do with it. That he summoned them and nourished them, that life without them was unthinkable. How to live free of their tugging? It was a longing. Like the Wind Rivers, snow sweeping in a broad upland into mist, the summit completely whited out. His *ghosthaus*.

Amazing how ghosts clung to suspects in a case. Maybe he'd talk about that on "The A.M. Show." Naw, he thought, bad for business. And the phone hadn't rung in weeks, except Follet wanting a chess game.

In the mirror he watched the dust floating in the sunlight flooding his office. He had been conversant with ghosts and now he needed rest. It had not occurred to him till now how troublesome it was working with people.

WIND news said Jennifer's attorney was demanding that the

case be thrown out of court. She was waiting in the county slammer for something to break. She'd wait a long time.

Meanwhile, White Bear was in Rawlins doing two years for something else.

And then there was Frampton, Frampton the spook, the closest thing there was to a ghost. Frustrated at not being able to pin Al Ling's murder on him, Follet had canned him for irregularities in his handling of the case. Frampton'd hired a lawyer and raised a stink. He was even a guest on "The A.M. Show." But then it had all died down. Frampton was since rumored to be up in Jackson working as a big-shot lawyer's bodyguard. D. W. Ling knew but wasn't talking. D. W. had never even appeared in court. He'd sent his lawyer, a Chinese kid from San Francisco, who'd argued that the old man knew nothing of his nephew's connection with North Star. The Chinese community was deeply grieved, he'd said.

In Cheyenne the governor announced he would sell his interest in North Star. No further comment was forthcoming.

Manetti never surfaced. For six months Manetti was everywhere, like geology, assuming the proportions of Howard Hughes, the Nevada lode, too big and otherworldly for folks in Wyoming. And the memory of Abe Marsh remained clean. His sister saw to that. The Siberian man-thing in a granny dress, she acted the part of Cattle Kate, done wrong and outraged. Her attempt to re-open the case against Frampton was pending. Earlier, she'd initiated construction of a line of condos close to the Little Big Horn. A tourist gold mine, she argued, a boon to the economy.

Adrian smiled at that over dinner. She wore a Mexican blouse and necklace and new boots, and she smelled good. "C'mon," she said, "how'd it go?"

"I told you."

"Did anybody call in?"

"Some woman complained about the government killing off

the herds. Hagar cut her short. Then a rancher called in. He wanted the horses shot. Said he was going out of business."

"Because of wild horses? Come on! It's beef prices."

"And interest rates, that's what I told him."

"What did he say?"

"Nothing. He just stayed on the line, breathing. It sounded like just before a fight when a guy runs out of words. He's either gonna swing or cry."

Adrian sipped her oolong tea. "A lot of ranchers are going under."

"It'll come back," said Boyd.

"I don't know."

She looked like she could see the future in the bottom of her cup. "This is the longest they've been down," she said. "You lose your stock and you never make it back. You have any idea how many ranchers work in the mines? They've had to leave their families. A bunch of them got trailers together in town. They work seven days a week and send their money home."

"Like the Chinese," said Boyd.

"Trouble with this country is we put all our eggs into energy. And when that fizzles, whaddya got?"

"Tourism," he replied.

Again she smiled. It was an old dialogue.

"And who'd ever visit this godforsaken hole?" he added.

She broke a fortune cookie, read her fortune, and set it on the saucer. "So when are you leaving?" she asked.

"I don't know."

"Exxon's starting up their gas plant at LaBarge," she said. "They say it'll take five thousand workers."

Boyd shook his head. "I'm thinking of going into radio. I want Hagar's job."

Adrian sighed. "Anyway, a lot of Texans are coming to town. It's gonna be crazy for a while. You should get a lot of business."

Boyd nodded. "Divorce, mostly."

"You ought to be pretty good at that," she said.

Boyd watched her for a second. She was hunched forward with the cup halfway to her lips, grinning, but her eyes were dead serious. Suddenly he saw her as a much older woman. He had to say something quick; he was supposed to.

"What do you want me to do, stay here and grow old? Get buried together up on Boot Hill? I don't belong here. What are you going to do, run a sheep ranch after your dad dies? I don't fit into that."

"Then run for sheriff," she said.

Boyd slapped his shirt pocket for a cigarette. Six weeks and he still had a craving. Dammit, he thought, I don't smoke.

He drank water. "I don't know what I'm gonna do."

"Boyd," she said, sitting back in the booth, "what do you want?"

She sounded like Doloras. He watched to see if she'd go on and, when it looked as if she wouldn't, he opened his hands and shrugged.

"What are you scared of?"

He picked up the salt shaker, sprinkled some on the back of his hand and licked it. "Missing something," he answered.

"Missing what?"

"Where I'd be if I weren't here, I guess."

"You know what that is? That's death. You're using the *idea* of a place to keep me out."

"Well, whatever it is, I don't need you to tell me."

"Yes, you do," she said. "In fact you've already decided to stay."

"How do you know?"

"Trust me. You wouldn't go on radio if you weren't trying to get known."

"Getting known in Medicine Dog," he said.

"You could do worse."

He rubbed his temples, staring at the thin strip of paper on her saucer. It was time to show up, he thought, to finally arrive, to be here. And what did that mean? All he could think of was that he was safe in this world. Here he was sitting with a woman whose beauty was coming to him in waves of self-disclosure, waves from far out over the desert, from the Pacific, that hung in his mind like grapes. Tomorrow when he opened his eyes he'd be in Medicine Dog, Wyoming, a lover of sports and personal intrigue. Someone obsessed with mystery, who refuted solutions.

She was watching him. "Are you through?" she asked.

The whole thing had been a dance, he thought. The slow turning toward the rest of his life. It would be fruitful because he was safe. Much of the time he would not know that but he knew it now.

As they got up to leave he reached for her fortune. But she was too fast. "None of your business," she said. When he tried taking it from her, she popped it in her mouth. "What does it say?" he asked.

She swallowed it, then turned to him at the door and kissed him, a powerful, full-bodied kiss, her tongue lashing his clenched teeth.

Outside it was raining, just as promised. Hot rain smelling of sage and asphalt, the steam hanging like angels. Rain reaching out of the sky like great spouts of grace, the light vaulting and otherworldly, the earth clean again.

Back at her place they made love while the rain passed over. Soon the sun set and the fireworks began, hours of it, the whole town sweet with cordite. "Come here," she said, "you've got to see this."

They stood on the porch clasping the railing and craning their necks. The entire sky was a basket of flowers, the petals blooming from deep space. "Jesus," he said. He was shivering with light.